Penguin Books
Blood in the Rain

MW00720940

Margaret Barbalet was born in Adelaide in
1949 and spent the next ten years in rural
Tasmania. She has since lived in Adelaide,
Port Moresby, Bathurst and Canberra.
Throughout being a shop assistant, a student,
and an intermittent public servant, she has
persisted in writing fiction. She has had short
stories and two histories published, the latest
being *Far From a Low Gutter Girl*. She is
married with three young sons and is working
on her third novel.

MARGARET BARBALET

BLOOD IN THE RAIN

PENGUIN BOOKS

Published with the assistance of the
Literature Board of the Australia Council

Penguin Books Australia Ltd,
487 Maroondah Highway, P.O. Box 257
Ringwood, Victoria 3134, Australia
Penguin Books Ltd,
Harmondsworth, Middlesex, England
Penguin Books,
40 West 23rd Street, New York, N.Y. 10010, U.S.A.
Penguin Books Canada Limited
2801 John Street, Markham, Ontario, Canada L3R 1B4
Penguin Books (N.Z.) Ltd,
182-190 Wairau Road, Auckland 10, New Zealand

First published by Penguin Books Australia, 1986

Copyright © Margaret Barbalet, 1986

All Rights Reserved. Without limiting the rights under copyright reserved
above, no part of this publication may be reproduced, stored in or introduced
into a retrieval system, or transmitted, in any form or by any means
(electronic, mechanical, photocopying, recording or otherwise), without
the prior written permission of both the copyright owner and the above
publisher of this book.

Typeset in Goudy Old Style by Midland Typesetters, Maryborough
Made and printed in Australia by
The Dominion Press-Hedges & Bell, Maryborough, Victoria

CIP

Barbalet, Margaret, 1949-
  Blood in the rain.

  ISBN 0 14 008944 6 (pbk.).

  I. Title.

A823'.3

Publication assisted by the Literature Board
of the Australia Council, the Federal Government's
arts funding and advisory body

For Jack

ACKNOWLEDGEMENTS

Many friends have encouraged me to persist in writing fiction. In particular I would like to thank Sara Dowse, Dorothy Johnston and Elizabeth Tombs for their comments and company over the past five years. I would also like to acknowledge Kay Ronai of Penguin who kept in touch during the final revision, Carla Taines for her cheerful editing and the Literature Board for a Writer's Grant in 1984.

'Save Me' by Joan Armatrading reproduced by kind permission of Essex Music of Australia Pty Limited.

And as each and all of them were warmed without by the sun, so each had a private little sun for her soul to bask in; some dream, some affection, some hobby, at least some remote and distant hope which, though perhaps starving to nothing, still lived on, as hopes will. Thus they were all cheerful, and many of them merry.

Thomas Hardy, *Tess of the d'Urbervilles*

Intimacy and affection
frozen
in this game of chance
I forfeit
full hand of love
with no counters
like a moth
with no flame
to persuade me
like blood in the rain . . .
running thin—

'Save Me', words and music by Joan Armatrading

1

Step, step, step.

It was sunlit and warm and the main street seemed to stretch a long way. Jessie looked down at her feet encased in blue shoes, too tight at the toes and worn at the heels. How many small steps she wondered. The shadow darted ahead. She had to hurry to keep up with mother who strode ahead, grey cotton skirt rustling about her long legs. Jessie's short plump legs beat fast under her cotton smock. How many steps – step, step, step, and the legs in the blue shoes obeyed resolutely and marched bravely on behind the shadow. She began to feel prickly under her old straw hat. No matter how quickly the blue feet went, they were still losing ground; mother strode further ahead and the street seemed just as long.

They arrived at the bakery. They stepped under the verandah. How different it was! A dark world, a giant's gloom. All the way down the road splinters of sun had poked through the straw hat. Now the hat was swallowed by the verandah's shade. Where was the shadow? She stood still, considering the discovery. The angular shape that had darted ahead all the way up the hot street had disappeared under the green verandah distantly visible, sky-high. Mother was already opening the door of the bakery. Jessie caught the weight of the door and followed.

The blue shoes were invisible in the shade, but they walked behind the grey skirt to the counter.

The bakery had bow-fronted windows, inside which were displayed different fancy loaves, all far above the straw hat. Vast dim space drifted above the shelves; a long, long way off was the planked wooden ceiling. At the back of the shop the floor was raised several feet and there were wooden steps. Jessie sat on the steps. Mother had her hands on the loaf on the counter; the baker was laughing. Familiar smells came from behind the steps. The image of 'bread' slowly presented itself under the straw hat like a bubble rising in honey. A series of pictures appeared in slow succession: crumbs sticking to the plate; flat brown flaky crumbs sticking to a licked finger. Mother's hand holding a knife and Stephen's plate extended for another slice; slices of bread falling one upon the other on the table. Flaky crumbs stuck on the finger. Bread. The whole shop was hot and sweet with the smell. It seemed that the air itself was made up of the smell, just as the shelves and corners in the shop were lightened with dusty flour. Would she and mother be covered in the thick hot bread smell? Mother appeared as usual; tall and cool, a beautiful distant creature whose hand was difficult to grasp because of the long legs that moved so swiftly. Suddenly Jessie realized that the baker had turned and was laughing at her as she sat on the steps. She ran to the grey skirt which was already moving towards the door.

'Don't dawdle Jessie.'

They moved into the hot street again.

Someone, not mother, gave Jessie bread. Stephen. She was in the cot, wet, and irritable with hunger. Father lifted her out and sat her on his knee and Stephen handed her the bread. The terrible crying stopped. Stephen often fed her. Sometimes mother was there, but though she might sometimes see Stephen she never saw Jessie.

2

Father was the one who sang; mother the one who sighed. Mother was beautiful; father was there.

Mother was the back bent over the sewing machine in one corner. Father the one who lifted Jessie in the air and who slept all night (one night) in the yard. The yard was stones and dust. Jessie had a corner. She would squat in the corner and watch mother hanging out washing.

Jessie was walking behind the hotel. To one side of the path was a ditch. The path was gravelled with small cold red stones that marked her feet, but would they keep her feet on the path? The ditch followed beside her. White grass sprouted from each bank so that the bottom of the ditch could not be seen but the banks were wet and slippery. She saw her legs slipping down the bank, flailing in the grass, the smock covered in mud – but after that? How would the world appear from the bottom of the ditch? At last the ditch disappeared, ending in a horrible brown stain on the wall. The feet stopped, mesmerized by the stain: it ran from the mouth of the ditch.

Jessie was waiting for Stephen by the wall at the back of the hotel on the corner. The wall sloped up the hill to the corner of the street and then ran along to the back of the two-storeyed hotel. She was waiting in the western sun. The weeds at the foot of the wall grew in abundance, paspalum and soursobs in tufts and clumps. The wall stretched up and up, so far above her head that to look at the top which was edged with dusty red bricks she felt she must fall over backwards. The sun beat against the wall of biscuit-coloured stone warming her dress. She put out her hand to touch the wall. The hand was smaller than the stone embedded in the mortar daub. The hand moved to the next stone and was lost inside its edge again. She tried again advancing her hand along the wall, fingers spread-eagled

3

like a starfish but the hand was still too small for any stone. How hot it was! And where was Stephen? She felt trapped between the sun and the wall. What if the sun moved closer? She would be scorched like an ant. She squinted at the sun. He seemed to have his eye on no one but her. Where could she run to? The wall stretched ahead. Then she remembered that half-way along was the gate to the stables at the back of the hotel. She sidled along the foot of the wall. The sun remained, unblinking, beating down on her hair. Now she could see the distant edge of the gates and the gatepost built of red bricks. She inched along, not daring to look at the sun whose hot rays fingered her back. At last she reached the gates and could see into the brick-paved courtyard. A man had his back to her, he was washing a horse with a brush and bucket. Jessie stood transfixed by the size of the horse's wet and muscled legs. The man was a clown-like puny creature next to the horse. He was bending beneath the horse whistling into the silence. She couldn't go into the yard. She edged her way past the gate where a long stream of water was slowly advancing. She had forgotten the malevolent sun.

Suddenly she remembered Stephen. He would be cross because she didn't know where he was. She came to the end of the wall and the sun was cut off; the height of the hotel cast a shadow across the road and up the opposite bank. Down the dark length of wall she saw a figure waiting. It was Stephen! She ran towards him, he turned, and breathless, she collided with him.

'Where were you? I've been waiting for hours.'

She stopped. Hours? 'The sun was going to get me.'

'The sun couldn't get you, silly!'

He marched off and she walked behind him in grateful silence.

They were going to the wharf. From the hotel the flat grey rippled water could be glimpsed, but Stephen, much to Jessie's admiration, always made going to the wharf a complete expedition. They marched together out of the shadow cast by

4

the hotel, down through a short street which led onto the southern end of the wharf behind the interlocked railway tracks and the great sheds. Now the river was gone, hidden by the grassy rise, but the sound of the wind betrayed it. Jessie, her eyes on Stephen's resolute legs, thought they would never reach the top. Suddenly they were over and the wind seized their hair and shook their clothes.

At their feet lay the wharves, a mysterious organized area of railway trucks, sheds and oily pools of watery sky. Today was Sunday but during the week it was a busy place, for what purpose Jessie knew not, although Stephen, when asked, assumed a casual knowing air. The river meant nothing to Jessie and little more to Stephen. It was there, theirs; it would always be. Perhaps the river began far away, maybe even beyond the borders of the province in the inland; they only knew it ended here beside their sea. They knew nothing of the scene in another age when the wharf was busy every day of the week; when steamers carried so much cargo to and from the wharf that the little railway running along the main street was described (in letters to the paper by certain irate local citizens) as causing intolerable delays to commercial affairs. The river had been the life of the town, and children four decades ago could have watched fencing-wire and beer being loaded onto steamers and barges and, weeks later, have seen the same boats returning, loaded with wool bales from the inland, the vast spaces that connected the province with the rest of the continent. In another age, a silent knot of townsfolk had seen another depression arrive, had watched as the ship-building works were piece by piece dismantled and shipped away further up river to another town, leaving the foundry site empty and desolate and men out of work all over the town. Jessie never knew how families lugging a few bundles had, one by one, shifted on, leaving the silent streets, to look for work elsewhere. She could not know that a few families (the worst it was said) stayed on, improvident and hopeful, despite the gradual loss of their livelihood. They clung on in tiny shacks around the outskirts of the town, despised by the prosperous farmers of the nearby hills and disliked by the shrewd traders of the main street with whom they had close financial involvements. Now and then, the fathers in these families would receive a few days' work in one of the small shipyards.

If, as now, walking with Stephen's comforting presence close at hand, Jessie had encountered a massive grey wall of hessian blocks, each one higher than her head and higher than Stephen's shoulders, she would know that the grey blocks contained wool: Stephen had told her so. But that, to Jessie, was not connected with the wide heavily laden barges she and Stephen had once watched making their slow way down the river, low in the grey water. Jessie had been born on the river but the flocks, the farms and the steamers, and the trade on the river which had been the life, and now, the slow death of the town meant nothing to her.

Stephen was moving round the wool bales, patting each one authoritatively. Jessie put out her own hand but did not want to touch; they were so massive that she felt they must disapprove of a hand so small. So they idled across the gravelled yards between the sheds until they reached the wharf.

Jessie loved nothing so much as that moment: stepping from yard to wharf. Her feet, smaller than Stephen's and far smaller than mother's could provoke recognition from the wharf; no matter how quietly she stepped the wharf gave back a different sound, quite different from the sound made walking on the gravelled yard. She stepped backwards and forwards again and again, arms outstretched, eyes alight, just to listen to the hollow sound the feet made on the wharf. Nearly as delightful was the sense of suspension. The first step on to the wharf was still a step on land; the river began some distance out. But the timbers she was on led right out above the water and if she took only four steps, straight along one board, she would be able to see the water winking back between the timbers.

6

Treasuring every step, she moved slowly out. Ahead lay the vast expanse of grey water moving slowly out to sea between low grey and green banks. On a calm day, a puff of wind could make the whole surface ripple; a shivering would creep from wharf to island. Today, a strong breeze stroked the river alive, ripples and swells patterned its pelt but beneath it all the majestic body rolled, trailing what velvet of weeds and drowned timbers towards the sea.

Beyond the river to the east there was an island; to the west, low-lying marshy ground, dotted with clumps of reeds and twisted paperbarks. Beyond the tangled scrub could be glimpsed the bright white tops of the sandhills up which both sere and verdant plants crawled in ambitious assault. But always the summit of the sandhills emerged white and triumphant.

Beyond the sandhills, hidden from the town, was the ocean. The traveller to the town, when he was first alone with the silence of his thoughts, would suddenly become conscious of a far-off muffled roar. Then he would notice it at every turn, tunnelling and tunnelling, without cease. If the traveller stayed overnight in the town he would fall asleep to the distant pounding; it would become part of sleep itself. Next morning, when the breakfast clatter had subsided, he might hear the sea again, although, very often, the patient beating of endless waves would be blocked out by the shunting of trucks on the wharf, or the arrival of a slow train at the long platform in the main street in the town. If the traveller stayed for years he would become like the inhabitants of the tiny town: he would not hear the sea. Immediate sounds would block it from the ear, but it would remain nevertheless on the periphery of the mind, some forgotten drumming in the blood, to be missed and craved further inland.

Stephen and Jessie did not hear the sea now as they sat on the edge of the wharf. Stephen sat right on the heavily timbered edge which was raised a few inches above the general level of the wharf floor, but he would not let Jessie sit right on the edge.

Jessie stared at him mutinously from where she stood a few inches from the edge. Stephen's motives sprang from brotherly affection; although he would allow Jessie to explore the wharf and play on slips (to say nothing of equally perilous games amongst the reeds) he had been told not to let his sister too near the edge; so honourable if inconsistent, he did not.

'Father said, Jess,' he reminded the angry face. Jessie did a little dance from foot to foot.

'Father said, father said.'

She lay down on the comfortable boards so that her eyes and nose looked down into the water but she still was not 'close to the edge'. A massive supporting pile lay near her left shoulder. It was encrusted with families of tiny silver snails and where it entered the water it had a green slimy skirt, that independent of wind and river drifted this way and that beneath the transparent surface. Jessie was wondering dreamily where the pile went. It seemed just to dissolve in the water, and although her eye could see the coarse wood for a few inches beneath the surface, beyond that – nothing – the eye must return defeated to the inscrutable rippling surface.

'I saw a fish!'

'There!'

Jessie stared obediently into the water. Where was the fish? She thought she saw it, but no, it was not the fish.

'There!'

Jessie turned quickly, but the fish had gone. She wondered whether it had slid back underneath the wharf to that dark jumbled cave of rocks and water; the area they could walk over so quickly, poised high and dry above that murky dark. She turned her head to look along the edge of the wharf. It seemed to stretch forever in a long vanishing line to meet the lapping river. There were several boats tied up at the wharf: a wool barge with deck built out over the water in a long curve from stem to stern, a paddle steamer, shabby paint peeling from the cabin and a small ketch, bobbing on the water. Overlooking the wharf, like a man's peaked cap, was the enormous open-sided shed, which always made her feel like running or skipping or shouting; not a place to dawdle.

'Jess!'

She jumped.

'Let's play the moving game.' So they sat together, carefully looking only at the water lapping past in an endless chain of ripples and presently the wharf began to move steadily down the river, two small passengers aboard beneath the vast grey arc of the sky.

She was a grain of sand at the centre of pearly layers of warmth. Warmth was centred around her back and knees. She lay in bed in the dim smoky room while the fire winked and died in the grate and the shadows shrank down the walls. Layers of warmth came from the blankets on the little cast-iron bed in the corner of the room: the room itself was a small dark capsule of warmth within the tiny house which stood alone against the battering wind and rain; the oyster's shell shut tight against the desolate moaning of wind and water.

Father came in and began to undress. Mother was already in bed, her face to the wall, only a patch of dark hair visible between blanket and pillow. Jessie, half-lulled to sleep by Stephen's quiet breathing next to her on the pillow, loved to watch mother and father undress across the room. Father took off his coat and hung it on a hook on the wall. Then he sat on the edge of the sagging bed so that the mattress bulged out beneath the springs. Mother, muttering angrily, pulled at the blankets that had been dislodged from her shoulders. He began to unlace his boots, turning back the cuffs of his trousers to do so. Jessie, who could not yet unlace boots, watched as if a charm were being unravelled in the shadowy room as the laces flew from one side of the boot to the other. At last they could be prised off and thrown at the foot of the bed. He stood

9

unsteadily and put one clumsy thumb inside his braces and took them off each shoulder so that they hung down on either side. Unaware of Jessie, but from sheer force of habit, he turned his back on their bed and began to unbutton his trousers to reveal yellowed woollen underpants. Jessie stared fascinated by the massive twin legs that stood solidly on the wooden floorboards while the arms unbuttoned the shirt and placed it on the bedrail next to the trousers. In yellow flannel shirt and underpants he went across to the fire and raked the coals so that darkness retreated for a moment, then advanced across the walls and covered the room.

She could hear voices at the end of a long burrow of sleep. Blank walls of sleep began to thin a little and somewhere in her head a round patch of light appeared. Words formed in the mouth of the tunnel. Father was talking to mother. The room was quite dark. She felt the dark drowsiness closing in on the patch of light.

'No, Charlie, no.'

Sleep closed the burrow; darkness and oblivion shut out the voices.

Stephen could take her to the beach. It was a clear winter day, rare for the town which usually spent winters beneath a pale grey sky across which cloud tussled from the east and from the west, each bringing squalls, competing to see which could most needle the flat surface of the river and imprison indoors the housewives of the town. Mother, sitting on the bed sewing, glanced at the departing figures.

'Take care of her, mind.'

She bent her slender neck over her sewing again. We're reflections in a dirty mirror Jessie thought.

They walked to the road that led to the sandhills, to the south. Stephen knew the way and walked quickly but Jessie's shorter legs soon lagged behind, and as always, Stephen, contrite, would slow down for several minutes, while she, grateful for his concern and not wanting to concede the slower pace that fewer years of age brought, would attempt to move her legs at a pace that she imagined to be his. But after a few minutes his excitement would lengthen the gap between them again and Stephen would have to resort to stopping and waiting for his sister every few minutes.

They left the road and the river was hidden by a wall of reeds moving and whispering each time the wind passed over their light heads. A low marshy swamp had to be braved. Reeds and stunted red and orange samphire dotted the stretches of water, so that they had to pick their way carefully from island to island, explorers following a fragile chain. As they walked, birds started from their path, like the spray flying before a boat. Overhead, flocks of gulls kept up a desolate mewing. Jessie stopped to look back. She could hardly see the town. It appeared no more than a small huddle of brown buildings surmounted by the thin spire of the flagstaff. She looked ahead. Stephen, unaware that she had stopped, continued methodically onwards across what seemed to her an endless territory of water-locked rises. She began to scramble after him, reckless across the pale blue patches of water, running across the endless marsh. It was rimmed with sandhills to the south; to the north by the low rise that marked the border of the town and beyond that, blue in the distance, the hills that stretched in an arc some distance from the town. Through the clearness of the day Jessie and Stephen advanced with beating hearts: small dots under a vast oblivious sky.

Stephen reached the edge and turned to watch his sister as she covered the last few yards towards the warm safety of the sandhills.

'Good on y', Jess.' Her shoes were no wetter than his own and her heart glowed. She would always be safe with him, he was tall and would protect her, cherish her and what was sometimes most important of all, wait for her feet to catch up.

The sea gew louder and louder as they began the trek through the sandhills. It was an undulating landscape, a country buried by sand; pale green grass with a silvery gloss sprouted even now on the tops of dunes. Half-submerged by sand, bushes, the size of houses, with flat green leaves and small cream flowers tumbled in abandonment down the slopes. Louder and louder grew the sea. Jessie thought they might see it as they trudged to the top of the crest, but, no, they had to begin a long descent into a hollow, where broken shells crunched beneath their feet and the wind was still. They were in the middle of a vast unmoving speckled pit; behind them broken tracks in the sand, ahead, the smooth surface and the sea drumming in their ears.

Now they reached the top and could see the wet sand and the tumbled lines of breakers. The sea was reluctant to allow even a strip of sand to remain and might at any moment snatch away the beach. Might not those foaming claws rush in up the dune to their feet and force them to run? She stayed seated on top of the dunes while Stephen ran down, arms outstretched to the line of wet sand. He became a tiny speck shouting at the hissing ocean.

She was alone in an enormous windy world. Sand blew off the dune in fitful gusts and all around her the silver grass hurried about like spiders before the wind. Banks of cloud edged across the hills behind the town. And in front of her feet was the sea, never pausing in its beating and tossing.

Suddenly she noticed a pattern in the sand at her feet, a perfect curve beneath a quivering grass scimitar. It was a groove carved by the compass of the grass. Looking about, she found dozens of similar marks, where the wind had worked the fabric of the dune. She ran her fingers along one. In a trace the perfect line vanished and thousands of grains of sand tumbled in disorder. She ran her fingers over another groove. Irritated, the moving tip of the grass began to move again and again, re-carving that circumference, moving the tumbled disorder beneath a relentless pen. Moments later the sand was lettered again. What did it mean? What did the wind write amongst those grains? She would ask Stephen. She climbed to her feet and started to run, stumbling and laughing in the wind, to the tiny figure below. But when she reached him the force of her pell-mell descent kept her running past him, so that he grabbed her hands just as her feet were covered by the rushing surf.

'Stephen,' she began.

'Jessie, Jessie!'

She began to laugh. He was turning her round and round, holding her hands.

'Stephen.'

The wind blew her words away. She couldn't ask him. She was spinning, her plaits flying out behind her, her wet shoes flying over the gleaming sand, and her laughter as loud in her ears as the never-ending pulse of the sea.

In one of his hands lay the apple, in the other the knife. Jessie watched as the apple fell apart, the neat intricacy of the seeds revealed in the centre.

'I'm bigger so I get three-quarters.'

He looked sideways as he said it, knowing that it was new logic.

'That's not fair.'

There, she had said it as he knew she would. For a minute there couldn't be arguments for they were too hungry, their mouths both full. Apple forced its way down Jessie's throat and as the chunks went painfully down her words flared as furiously up.

'Father said to share, Stephen. You're not sharing!'

He was silent but provokingly ate another quarter of apple.

'Greedy-guts!'

Hot tears began behind Jessie's eyes. Perhaps she could kill him with his knife – dead.

They rolled in the dust at the foot of the tank, scratching and kicking. Never had she wanted so much to hurt him.

Mother was shouting from within the house and they stopped and retreated to the shade of the tank. Stephen found the knife and the apple in the dust and washed them under the tap. He shared it with her, making her dusty face soften despite the tears drying on her cheeks in the hot February morning.

Eating her fair share she looked at his face. Where had all that temper gone? She hadn't meant to kill him, had never even lunged for the knife, but scratching and kicking had seemed only a minute ago, to be sweet, to be perfect. Now he had a scratch on his neck and she knew when he finished his half-apple, he too would still be hungry.

She would grow up and be rich and give him apples, all to himself, every day.

A day came that was different – a day when the yard seemed bare and large and, heaven knows, far more dull; Stephen left for school.

It seemed terribly unfair to try to play marbles by herself but she did in the end try. The little glass balls with their chipped surfaces rolled in the dust towards the hole. She won all the games and was bored.

She wandered over to the fence, then the gate. I'll go to the school she decided and see if he can come home again and not go. Never go again.

It seemed strange to be thinking of walking to school all by herself. She felt very grown-up idling into the house for her hat. On his bed, father lay snoring away the dusty heat of the morning. Mother was out shopping or she might be visiting a friend.

You walked down the road and turned left. Would no one see? She half expected someone to shout. But the landscape seemed not to notice. She reached the school at last. No one was about. Wrapping her fingers over the top of the gate she stared at the deserted yard where there were two pepper trees. On the verandah of the school-house, a canvas water-bag as if to deny her existence, swayed in time to some invisible touch.

Suddenly a bell rang so that she jumped and had hardly overcome her surprise when a stream of children burst out of the little box-like school-house and ran into the yard. Some of the girls looked like grown-ups. They walked together with their arms around each other's waists.

And then in the distance she saw a group of boys and yes – her heart leapt with joy – there was Stephen, his face so familiar and nice, nicer than any of the others. In a minute he would see her and they would go away together. She waited in the sun. He must see her soon!

The big girls were skipping now; the spinning rope tossing out the chant; words flying from the ground like chips axed from wood.

This year,
Next year,
Sometime,
Never.

Why didn't he see her? Her heart began to jolt like a parcel in a cart. He was walking away from the school-house towards the far fence with his hands in his pockets listening to another boy who walked with him. She couldn't go in and get him she knew. Unless he saw her, she felt her heart might simply break; snap its strings and then what? Would everything roll out and be thrown about like the contents of a broken parcel in a cart? What would become of her without him?

Big House,
Little House,
Pig sty,
Barn.

There they had finished!
But now she heard the bell begin to ring and saw all the

children stream back into the school again, and he was lost forever.

Mother was going away on the train. Somewhere, a long way away there was a city, and mother was going there. Stephen and Jessie and father stood on the platform together, and a little apart, mother stood in a new pale blue dress and hat. It was windy on the exposed platform and one hand was constantly in use, steadying the large new hat which lifted perilously every time a gust of wind caught the brim. Other passengers clustered further down the platform. The train was late.

Father edged closer to mother.

'You'll be back in a week then, Clare?'

'Of course I will.' Mother had one hand on the hat, the other pulling at the waist of the new dress.

'I'll be staying, you know, with Kathleen.' Father nodded.

A long way down the line the train had appeared. The train was a mere speck, then the speck was swallowed by a toy train, and finally, the noise of pistons and wheels and the smell of smoke became a real train that rushed along the track and jerked to a clanging halt. A long hiss escaped. Passengers alighted and others climbed aboard. Mother kissed Jessie and Stephen on the cheek, one hand still on the hat. Mother and father. Jessie remembered the large voices in the little house. Good. No more fights. Father made to take her in his arms.

'Charlie.'

Mother pressed his arm away. They exchanged a peck, then mother picked up the bag and climbed into the carriage. Father's trousers were creased and dirty and his coat was old and shapeless. He was unshaven beneath his hat. Jessie thought of the way mother had smelt a moment ago: fragrant and young. Mother's face appeared at the window. The men were putting back the canvas hose they had used to put water into the engine and the guard boarded the train. The train jerked. Everyone stood back and began to wave. Mother waved and Jessie and Stephen waved to mother. They waved the train away. The blue hat and mother vanished. Then as the train drew out, they waved to the other passengers and to the departing guard in the doorway at the back of the train until the whole line of carriages was once more a speck in the distance.

On the sloping beach near the foaming edge, a sandpiper scurried ahead over the gleaming sand. Jessie was walking backwards watching the sea erase their footprints. One wave meant that the impression became softened; two waves left a dimpled mark. Then there was nothing. Stephen was looking for shells. Saturday yawned ahead of them.

'Mother isn't coming back.'

Had she heard that? Mother not coming back, she thought wildly. 'How do you know?'

'I just know.' He was stooping to rescue a shell from the sea's flounce. 'It's five weeks.'

Jessie thought of mother. The sea rushed back and her footprint might never have been. Mother had become a small speck like the train itself. She tried to think what Stephen meant. Mother had had a new blue hat and it had nearly blown off on the platform.

Stephen stepped up to her, his feet wet, and opened his palm to show her what he had found. It was a mussel shell, the delicate halves hinged at the back, both pale yellow shells stained with colour, red with a butterfly's flash. He tore the halves apart and sent them skipping into the waves.

'We'll go fishing when I get her goin'.'

'Can we cook them? I'll cook.'

'Course we'll cook them.' Stephen scratched his leg and looked back at the boat. How to shift it. Cliff and Joe would have to help. And first they'd have to get the water out of her. Water lapped in a friendly way at his legs as he waded inside the boat. Behind this boat was a stretch of reeds where other boats waited, beached in the reeds like forgotten tombstones while the river idly pushed its fingers between timbers and paint, letting the sand settle gently on caulk and timber without distinction or haste.

The wharf was distant, deserted.

Jessie was spying on two swamp hens conspiring in the gossiping reeds. It was summer, certain and golden; mother, a vanished speck.

Suddenly the birds scurried away. Two women were advancing down the river bank, the sun catching their white dresses and parasols. They stopped. Jessie felt their eyes tighten on dark thoughts, secret seeds amongst the whiteness of their summer skirts, the fullness of their lacy hats.

'Hello Stephen, Hello Jessie. How are you?'

There seemed to be no answer to this question from knee-deep in the river. Stephen went slowly red, the boat fell from his hands as he stood up under the stares of the women.

There was a silence. How clean their dresses were! She had never seen such dresses, such layers and folds, such rows and rows of lace.

'When's Mrs Sheldon back, then?'

Jessie watched as Stephen's face struggled to find the lie. 'Soon.'

'Soon. But you don't know when?'

There was another silence. Finally, the taller of the two women tucked her arm through the other's elbow and they walked away talking together, twin white pendulums on a slow-ticking clock.

Stephen picked paint off the dinghy. He walked to the bank.

Jessie began to feel the afternoon's expanse and pleasure drain away.

'Don't you want to play here, Stephen?' He didn't answer, and after a moment, she splashed out of the water, and, her dress flapping about her wet legs, began to run after him.

'Come on Jess. And pull y'dress down.'

Stephen cross, black as a cloud.

The last blessing finished, the Church of England congregation of the little town began to move slowly out of the church. At the door a great knot formed on the gravel. Everyone needed to talk to the minister or at the very least, to his wife. The church door opened to the south and here the burghers stood in ecclesiastical gloom, the sun hidden by the high brown buttressed stone of their church. The autumn wind worried the grass outside the stone wall that ran right around the churchyard. Within the wall it was halcyon calm. Families trickled down the path, uncertain as water on stony ground. A few of the most distant began to venture a quiet remark or two about the sermon; opinion formed that, as usual, it had been poor. The children, who had been sitting in the church long enough to gain what they might have characterized (had they been profane) as an interesting insight into the meaning of eternity, edged along the path ahead of their parents, hurrying with care in their Sunday best past all the conversations, escaping into the sun.

'Unchurched!'

'Their mother may have taken them, Caroline.'

'Only to parade her hats.'

'You don't know. But perhaps', Miss Mary Crowther added, 'you should mention it.'

The adults too were dispersing now. When the crush had broken down a little, Miss Caroline Crowther allowed herself to cough and then beckoned the minister aside with an authority that she felt her age could allow her to exercise over a man of the cloth.

Miss Mary, younger and less assured at forty than her elder sister, waited a little to one side.

'Of course. Of course. You have the welfare of the children at heart.'

Caroline Crowther had not stopped.

' – the summer by the river. Directly we spoke to them they ran off. The girl was in rags. Indecently clad. Scratching. They're growing up like savages.'

The minister agreed. Yes of course Mr Sheldon should be helped. Perhaps there were relations. That uncle in the city, a Mr James, he was reminded. Miss Crowther, who had by now a sense of her own large part in other's destinies, wavered a little (from duty) and professed herself ignorant of the father's character but the children . . . Oh dear.

They walked together down the path past the red-leaved cotoneasters where the parishioners were dispersing home, on foot and by carriage, to Sunday lunch. Lunch, Miss Mary Crowther reflected, walking behind her sister and the minister, would be mutton, as usual, rather overdone.

2

Afterwards he remembered nothing of the journey, only its beginning and end.

The beginning had been Miss Dorothy James knocking at the door of their cottage and then sitting in the kitchen drinking a cup of tea and talking with father. He and Jessie had watched from the doorway. Jessie had begun to rock from foot to foot after a while but he had listened to the words between the strange woman and father. Father had crashed about in the little kitchen. He had stoked the fire. He had cleared the table. Then he and the strange woman sat down together, talking but becoming more unknown to each other with every minute that father's elbows rested on the table.

In the shop where they had gone together all the people had walked about like dolls or wooden soldiers before the tiny angry figure of Miss Dorothy James. He had stood behind her feeling smaller and smaller because she was so important. Never had he felt the town so much around him, staring and seeing. If he were a fish the town would slide so, over his scales, backwards like a knife. The town in the form of the draper himself, not one of the scowling assistants who had served him in the past, knew all about him by the time they had finished their shopping. The draper with a professional pursing of the lips had measured him, the tape in his pink hands. By the time the morning was over the draper knew the length of his legs and feet. He also knew the circumference of his head, the space behind his eyes.

He walked beside Miss Dorothy all the way home, in his new knickerbocker suit, clothes of a smartness and freshness that he could hardly believe. When she wasn't looking he even put his nose to his sleeve just to taste again the woollen smell. In his hand he carried a parcel wrapped around with string. On his head he wore a new straw hat and the straw was white and strong and shiny. Father's hat was greasy and smelt of father's head. He swung the parcel.

When he saw their tiny shabby cottage he thought of the house in the city, a treat waiting to be unwrapped. Inside the parcel, jolted unregretted all his old clothes.

The tram stopped and they stepped out into a world of blueness and shadow. High above the trees and roof tops was a black night sky, pricked with dim stars.

'We either have to walk back or on from the tram stop,' Miss Dorothy said to him. 'I always walk downhill.'

So the house must be over there, there among the anonymous fences and hedges. She took his hand and they crossed. The road, wide and deserted, seemed to cut a path through the sleeping houses, a bare swathe the colour of midnight that stretched away behind them, climbing up and up as if it could lead into the night sky at its end. He had known they were climbing in the tram and he reflected to himself that they must be on the outskirts of the city. The tiny woman, who it appeared was a cousin, walked beside him in silence on the asphalt footpath. He had not liked to ask what a cousin was, afraid he might discover that he was ridiculous for not knowing. For he had understood this much from his father's remarks, that he was also her cousin and how could he ask, he a boy of eight, grown-up compared to his sister, ask another to tell him what he, in part, was?

They stopped at a corner and she ushered him in through a heavy wooden gate that was set in a hedge. Even at night he saw that it was the sort of hedge that would bar everything. The only way to the house was through this gate. Now they were through the thickness of the bristle-short hedge and he felt gravel crunch under his feet. They walked up steps to a front door. Inside, a light burned in a distant room. They stood in silence after Miss Dorothy rang the bell. From a long way off he heard footsteps come deliberating towards the door, stopping twice to turn on lights and then through the coloured glass around the door he saw a tall shape begin to turn the key and then the door was opening on the tallest man he had ever seen who stood dividing the light square of the doorway. There was a column of light to his left and to his right and in the middle a pair of hooded eyes that looked at him from head to toe as though he were not dressed properly, not dressed smartly, not dressed in marvellous new clothes at all.

They went in after that, the tall man taking Miss Dorothy's bag. He asked her how the journey had been and she told him in a tired voice, a new voice. He walked behind them through the hall over squares of carpet with knotted borders, past etched prints in dark frames and chairs with claws extended on their legs, eternal talons. Mr James opened the second door and they went into a long room where a small fire huddled in a huge grate. Miss Dorothy touched his arm. He understood he was to sit in the small chair facing the fire between the two larger chairs. Mr James sat down and poked at the fire, replacing the poker in its stand with a small twist of his fingers.

Stephen wondered what he was supposed to say. Mr James was silent, staring into the ashes. The warmth of the fire made the night outside no longer adventurous but hostile. He felt sleep begin to steal along his legs.

'Dorothy will bring you some milk directly,' Mr James said. 'After your journey.'

Stephen smiled and then felt the smile die, unanswered. The hooded eyes merely looked at him again and then looked away into the grate.

Miss Dorothy brought him a glass of warm milk and he realized as he took the glass how empty he was. He drank without stopping until the glass was empty.

'You're not very well grown, are you,' Mr James said suddenly with a little smile as Stephen put back his glass on the tray.

'But a good forehead,' Miss Dorothy cried.

She sat opposite, almost flushed at her boldness.

'Irish vacuity, I predict.'

Stephen felt he might not have been there.

'I think that you should show the boy to his room. He's nearly asleep.' He looked at her in amusement.

'Make a silk purse out of a sow's ear tomorrow, my dear,' he added stirring his tea with concentration.

Miss Dorothy stood up suddenly and came over to Stephen's chair.

'There's no need to get emotional,' Mr James said raising his eyebrows so that he looked at her from an even greater distance.

'After all, what do you know about these matters?'

She looked out of the window at the garden's blackness. The boy sat frozen.

'I believe – ', she began. How to explain that she had felt compassion and a sort of hope when she had taken the children from the dreadful cottage. It had not been easy. He had handed her a cup of tea and so dirty was the cup that she could not decide in the dim light whether the line on the cup was a hair or a crack in the china. But she had rescued the children, arranged for the girl to go to an aunt, and brought the boy, poor frightened creature, back here.

24

'There's something fine about him.'

She looked at her father.

He got up, annoyed, and put his cup back on the tray.

'Good-night Stephen.'

She was as small as a child as she led him out of the room. They went down a long dim passage and opened one of many doors. The room was huge with a door in the far wall. In one corner was a large high bed. He was to turn out his own light.

When she had gone, shutting the door, he walked carefully around the room feeling its strangeness expand around him as her footsteps died away. The room with its old carpet and heavy chest of drawers, its few pictures too high for him to see, made him shrink even as he stood there in his socks. The ceiling seemed far far away. It was a room for giants. He tried to look at his face in the mirror on the chest of drawers but it was tilted too high and where he expected to see his own face, company of the best sort in the night silence all around him, he saw nothing except the reflected blankness of the wall above the bed.

He had never had such space around him. The room was bigger than the whole of the cottage where he had lived with Jessie and father. All that life, the town and the river seemed very distant as he climbed into bed. He lay in the soft coldness looking up at the light cord above his head. In the silence he heard a mopoke owl divide the night into past, present and future and listening, heard it again and again measure all the silence and strangeness of the house he was sleeping in.

He awoke to the sound of frogs. There was an open window high above the glass door. His light was off. Someone must have come in, in the night and turned it off. And his clothes were not as he had left them. They were neatly folded on a chair. Yet he was alone and the house was silent and empty. The scene of the night before, the tall man with hooded eyes, appraising him coldly before the fire, had dwindled to a memory. He stole over to the glass door feeling the threads of the carpet under his feet. The door was locked. But it looked out to a garden, a long stretch of forgotten grass which the morning sun had not yet combed. Dressing quickly, he decided he would find the frogs.

Opening the door of his room he tiptoed out into the dark length of corridor he had walked along last night. The back of the house must be the other way. He crept through the sleeping house to the door at the other end of the hall. It opened onto a back verandah, bare and cold with an ochre-red floor. As in the hall, here too there were doors everywhere, all shut. He looked back up the hall, feeling the trap of quietness poised all around him ready to snap and snare if he made one false move, opened the wrong door. But it was easy to tell which was the back door: it had a heavy square lock like the doors at home. That had been a house with no doors except front and back. You were in or out. To find out anything here he would have to risk opening these doors.

Outside in the first light he found all the doors of the morning open. On the back fence was a huge gum tree. Gravel paths wound away to a chook-house and two sheds, rain still pasting leaves to their wet iron roofs. He went around to the side of the house. Gravel crunched and would make tracks if you dragged your feet backwards. You could leave a dancing pattern of brown footprints.

At the end of the cold wall of the house he came out into the front garden. A small cushion of lawn dazzled him in the sunlight. In the lawn was a rockery containing a pond. Elaborate and ornamental rocks sheltered the water beneath its lace of wire. Flat lily leaves floated on the surface like ships that have long since forgotten their destination. A grotto shaded the far end of the pond; the morning sun swam, trapped in slow currents, on its rough ceiling.

Stephen sat on the edge of the pond and saw the shape of

his ears and head, his own shadow smooth away the reflected light and reveal the stems and mud. Into that shadow came a sudden memory of the summer's common reflection: two heads leaning over colder water, a faster current. The sun shone, warming the back of his neck. It seemed as though he had been here in this house forever, as though the town on the river had never existed. He looked at the familiar outline of his head and shoulders on the water's surface, and all at once the watery mirror seemed to show him past the surface brightness.

Jessie had cried when she said goodbye. But she had cried when he went to school. She always cried. She was too young. He wouldn't cry. What was the point? He was here in the sun. He would catch frogs.

Water gripped his arm to the elbow. He felt around on the floor in the depths of the pond. He couldn't see. Mud began to cloud the water. His fingers groped blindly, feeling stones and then touching something that moved in a panic like a finger evading his own. Through the mists of the water he saw a golden shape pirouette towards the lilies. So there were fish! Now he recognized other golden streaks, now he saw that the pond was a city of fish.

Suddenly, like a pulse, a frog hopped right into his hand. His fingers clamped around it. The frog slipped and convulsed and then trembled into stillness, water into ice. His left hand pulled his handkerchief from his pocket and both hands netted the frog, practised goalers working together.

It was a bigger frog than he had ever caught from the river. He put back the wire and walked through the paradise of gravel to the house.

Someone was up. In the kitchen he could hear noises. The smell of meat cooking followed him to his room and a sweet hunger began to sound his ribs. He put the frog, still wrapped in the damp white handkerchief, in the warm hollow at the centre of his bed and pulled the blankets up over it. It might blunder about there but it would merely discover the reaches of its prison.

He stood still in the centre of the room. It was not the room of the night before. At its centre he stood and he hugged his secret. The room was his and would serve his purpose. He went to the door and half opening it, waited, listening, his hair uncombed, his pointed face adrift with the intelligence of his ears. The house was huge and silent. Listening, he thought the house like a stone, a stone that you pick up from under water attracted by the colours that gleam, asleep on its roundness. Beneath the water it lay, orange and red, worth sliding your arm into any deep or slime. Anything might be there but you wanted the stone.

He was not supposed to explore. That he understood.

He crept down the hall, away from the back door. At the end of the hall, a door lay ajar and he glided around it. He could hear breathing as soft and regular as the sound of a curtain on a sill, lapped by the wind. Mr James lay asleep in a high bed against the wall. Stephen stared. A grey light lay over the room; shapes were softened and blurred. Waves of sleep were receding gently back across the room, the light seemed part of sleep itself, as little caring or formed as a cloud. But light glared in around the blind. What would happen if he awoke? He slept on and on.

There was a sudden sound from the bed. Heart thudding, Stephen fled down the passage to his own room.

Hungry and triumphant Stephen waited in the kitchen, watching the cook, out of the way. The kitchen was warm with a heavy mutton smell, and the cook, who had felt the cold of first light, watched the small curled shapes, glad to be close to the stove. The chops were small loin, poor, she thought, but tender, already browning, the tails curled by cooking and

28

the marrow tight within the bone. She moved the cover so that the flame retreated, cut, and went through the pantry to check the dining-room. The table was set with smooth linen, there was butter, marmalade and jam, both apricot and plum, with spoons beside each small dish, the bread on the breadboard, the places neatly laid with each table-napkin neatly furled within its initialled ring.

'Yes, it is ready,' she said, conscious that the child was still waiting, might be hungry. But he was not to eat until Mr James came in.

The room was long with diamond-paned French windows opening north onto the verandah, beautiful cool windows on a hot summer's morning but now, on a sharp early winter day it was gloomy so that the flat white tablecloth glowed in the centre of the room. She had forgotten the fruit. Going hastily to the kitchen she took down the silver bowl and selected two more apples from the pantry, rubbing them on the skirt of her apron.

'Here, you take these in,' and handing him the bowl she took the teapot out through the back verandah. Stephen saw the table and his own place laid at it.

At half-past eight, long after father, Dorothy came in to breakfast alone. Father had long ago declared that she was delicate. She needed early morning sleep. The life of father and daughter in this and everything else revolved around the mutual peripheries of each other's existence. Dinner conversation had always been occupied with hesitant consideration of those small matters that occur in a quiet domestic life. They never clashed: there were never large issues to be resolved; those questions of life which shape the human character never intruded at Lombard Avenue. Every minor issue was delicately broached, retreatingly suggested with verbal salutation and bowing gesture to the respondent. Alternative modes of action would be correctly assessed and the speaker having completed his pace would retire with delicate verbal tread. Finally both father and daughter would reach a decision, supposing themselves to be in agreement after discussion of a difference—but in fact no difference had ever occurred. No real discussion ever took place; there was no disagreement or extension of sympathy, no discovery with attendant fascination or withdrawal. No unpleasantness ever disturbed that minuet.

Choices were made, it is true, and very often they would be recalled on a later occasion as if to bring to mind for both speakers their earlier pact. No, Dorothy would announce to her father, she would not open the windows in the dining-room, because father, knowing the orange tree was in blossom outside, strongly scented, white and green near the glass, had decided that it made her cough. They would have discussed the orange tree one night, around the sparkling tablecloth, the garden locked outside the leadlights, dark and hidden, but the scent whispering in the room. The conversation had proceeded like countless others; like all others it had reached a quiet conclusion after the appropriate pauses, but because there was on this occasion (as always) no discussion, the appearance of conversation but not the essence, like a dance of the deaf with no beat; because there was never conflict, no jarring words ever breaking up their elaborate steps nor forcing themselves between the measure; because there was no passion, no disdain, no heat, there was also no harmony.

She went to the window. Through the glass was the orange tree, thick with white flowers in the morning sharpness of the garden. Each leaf glistened and with face close to the glass, each leaf was clear. She liked best, to stand back a little as she stood now, so that the different angles of the panes bent and caught the spray. She would leave the boy to father. He knew best. But she could teach him at least to fold his clothes and make his bed.

Mr James stood at the tram stop this early winter day, irritated beyond belief. The tram had begun its hissing descent down the hill. He had been made two minutes late by having to turn back at the gate and tell the child not to walk in the front garden and not to scuff the gravel. Bad manners at breakfast he had expected, but not the spoilation of his garden.

The road was wide and ordered, neatly edged by high green hedges or starkly painted picket and cast-iron fences. Behind each fence nestled a house with expansive verandahs sheltering mysterious and unknown family life. The front gardens were neat affairs, all raked gravel, tethered chrysanthemums and tiny unused lawns, like the best linen handkerchiefs, only for show. But at the back of the houses, by some oversight, there remained here and there a giant gum, dropping bark onto the lawn below. This crisp May morning the sun was caught, winking and sparkling in the glossy leaves at the end of each twisted bough, and in the park, a little further up the hill, parrots hung screeching to the underneath of the shimmering branches.

Several other men had arrived at the stop as the tram drew near. He knew Paterson, and they exchanged a brief greeting and a mutual raising of furled umbrellas. Others were known to him; they lived further up the avenue and being junior clerks in city offices expected no more than his acknowledgement of their polite greetings. The tram arrived with a hiss and a clang; they climbed aboard as they always did, and it jolted away, away from the spacious gardens and the comfortable houses on the slopes at the foot of the hills.

Inside the tram, the men sat in silence. Mr James gazed as he always did, out of the window at the houses and shops that bordered the road. There had not been good suburbs and good streets like Lombard Avenue in his youth: the road had stretched only into the bush. Occasionally out there you might, even then, have seen signs of civilization – a stump or a cattle-yard – but most of it was unknown and unclaimed.

Four decades before his birth, there had been only the restless trees and a newly charted sea, when from rocking decks, blue eyes and white hands set out to row, for the first time, towards that green and fragrant shore. The land (over which the tram now raced) had lain before the explorers: gentle slopes thickly covered with forests. But what forests! Thin trees and strange prickly shrubs with hard shiny leaves and obscure fruits; white trunks struggling in a disorderly scribble for the sky above; clumps of grass with leaves like weapons positioned like an army on the slopes. It was not in any sense the gentle woodland it appeared from the ships. But the early settlers had expected this. Their reading fortified them and they greeted the strange plants with a shout or a laugh. South Australia *would* be founded here, a place to surpass, they would wager, any other model province. Everything would be different here – it was a new experiment. Somewhere in the ship were geometric plans for this city and a plan, too, for the life and peopling of these streets. It was surprising that there had been such bickering and personal differences over the plans but that had been, after all, a world away, in the old world across the ocean and the stars.

White feet splashed recklessly ashore. The province was proclaimed and the women hushing their babies to listen to the speech knew they would never see that far-off country again. Those sails, behind the little crowd of hot settlers on the beach, would not sail home. They knew that there was a way inland to other cities, beyond the distant border of the province across the continent. But no one would ever find a way there, through those forests.

With the axe the settlers had founded a city. Trees had been hacked and felled and hewn into carts and houses to replace the first tents. Mile upon mile of the strange and useless trees were burnt for warmth in recurring dark winter nights.

Holding the next year's crop of babies away from harm, the women watched as the great trees creaked and bent and then, away from the running man and his puny axe, crashed to the ground throwing twigs and leaves on to their skirts, provoking the men to laughter and the watching babies to red-faced tears.

When those babies were grown they too would fell forests but further out. The city grew as babies were born; each soft tiny hand could mean a new street. But carried everywhere, like some indispensable Torah, on the back of carts, or hidden amongst sacks of chaff, amongst all the light political ideas that would blow away with each year, was the belief that this was a better place; they were a better people.

The tram stopped. Groups of men alighted and began to walk in twos and threes to their offices through the busy streets. Mr James set off, as he always did, along the northern terrace, then along the main thoroughfare towards his office.

The city was rich. In the whole province there was only one city, this city that echoed smartly to his well-polished shoes and spats. The names of the streets were carved into the stone pavement that he had walked over every day for forty years. The city was known by everyone; by young feet, by old feet, by mud-caked country feet, by ladies' feet, dainty and not to be stared at, by the bride's feet in new kid shoes. Everyone knew the city and called it that, just that, for confusion could not exist. There were no other cities, just villages and jumped-up towns, thinking of the pretension of a park, maybe by the river. He walked now between magnificent buildings but though they were tall stone structures it was because they were the second or sometimes third edifice on their site, because the city was alive and consumed itself in itself, that it was truly a city. Rich years had built these thoroughfares and wealth had brought electric light.

His parents had not been wealthy but comfortable, the backbone of the province he had always thought. Two brothers had followed his father into the building trade and had, with the years, achieved a comfortable bourgeois latitude; he would not mention his sister or her marriage to the Irishman, Sheldon.

He married late; the third daughter of a pastoralist, Miss Letitia Symes, a very good marriage. He had the satisfaction of knowing that his brother's wives were quite in awe of the new Mrs Theodore James and his parents acquired the habit of tucking themselves into the background on any family occasion in the hope that age and reticence could hide breaches over cake forks or the buttering of bread. He himself had begun as a clerk, was now head of the department. He reached the door of the building now, and paused on the step, remembering, he couldn't imagine why, the day he had first walked nervously through into the lobby. Although the lobby was a panelled cave, the step outside caught the morning sun, and was now adorned as usual with a succession of sartorial young clerks enjoying the warmth, the bustle of the street, a moment of illicit hesitation before entering.

'Morning Sir.'

And he had the pleasure of seeing several of them dart inside at his approach. He pulled off his black gloves. He could not build like his brothers: his hands were startlingly soft and white. Pens and paper had given them their creases, thousands of movements had formed their shape; his index finger was bent at the tip by years behind the nib. His left hand did nothing as well as hiding a page with a blotter; his right, crabbing a copperplate minute.

He began to climb the stairs, swinging his umbrella before him, pausing on the landing to catch his breath, his spats and shoes catching the light from the low window which served to illuminate the stairwell. He would not have electricity wasted in the office, and, in his opinion, it was wasted on the stairs. At length he reached his office and unlocked the door. He made a point of arriving before the rest of the staff, casting an aura of lateness about their punctual arrival. He put his umbrella and hat in the corner and hung his coat behind the door.

He went to the window and stood looking out across the

zigzag of roofs and chimneys towards the blue folds of the hills. There was no doubt Stephen would require very careful watching. There was so much in him that had never been checked, that had run into tangle, into extravagant leaf; dirty thoughts, bad impulses, tempers, tears, insolence, no doubt a passionate desire for his own way. He had succeeded with Dorothy. All the little crises had been met; she had learnt to obey, to accept, to listen.

Work came like a great machine and took his mind away from the boy. The green leaves of memory dried and hardened one by one, and finally hung like a withered fruit, unregarded on the bough. But at five-thirty the city began to slow, to fumble, to close down. Long after the other clerks had boarded train or tram to their separate homes he sat, as he always did at his desk, working with a straight back until the outline of the city through his window became indistinguishable from the evening sky. Only then did he take down his hat and umbrella from the wall, and, having carefully tidied his papers, he relocked the door and began his journey back through darkened streets to the house on Lombard Avenue.

3

She was not nice, not nice at all, Miss Dorothy. He wanted to lean across the table and spit out all over the clean cloth the anger he felt. He swallowed and it stuck in his throat. How could he have thought she was nice only yesterday? Her father was tall and she was very small. At first it had seemed right that she should be small, she seemed neat, all parts in order. But when she was angry, and she had often been angry, her brown eyes leapt out from behind her glasses and her thin body jerked like one of the drawings Jessie would do. Then the eyes magnified by the glasses would enlarge like snails bulging from their shells, waving about as if they would never retreat again.

They were having lunch. He had expected breakfast with Mr James to be difficult from the moment they sat down together. The table which was laid with so much beautiful food had been enshadowed. He sat there feeling his skin tighten, feeling as if he were a small fish that suddenly sees a long shadow drifting onto the sandy floor and too frightened to begin glancing upwards, sees it halt. And at moments during the porridge and the chops and eggs he had been caught, had been told not to gobble, to hold his toast with one hand *only* please. Then the shadowy eyes went back behind the paper and he was left in peace.

He had eaten a lot. His porridge had been so coated with sugar, it had not tasted like porridge at all. He had helped himself to jam and to honey. The honey was in a little pot exactly like a house. You took off the thatched roof of the house and there was the honey, filling the whole of the little house from wall to china wall. The spoon handle poked out near the brick chimney. He would have toast and honey every day so that he could lift off the roof of the little house.

After breakfast when he had gone out into the garden Mr James had told him he had no business to be there. Someone called Pat who wouldn't come until Friday would have to rake the paths. And it was all because of him.

After that he had begun to feel that the house was not like a stone with strange colours. It was like a stone always became after hours in your pocket: dull and dusty, like hundreds of other pebbles, like gravel. He sat at the table trying to eat his lunch. The voice went on and on. He wondered how she found time to eat. This voice never stopped.

'Elbows off the table.'

'Cut that: don't put all that in your mouth at once.'

'Don't talk with your mouth full.'

He had been about to ask for some more bread but stopped.

'Don't clank.'

'Don't hold your knife like that.'

'There's no need to gobble.'

'Elbows at your side when you eat.'

'Don't speak with your mouth full.'

He sat back and looked at her dancing knife and fork.

'Elbows *off* the table.'

'Sit up straight.'

'Please *may I*: that's the way to ask.'

At home they had always eaten in silence, concentrating around the table. One end of the table held tins and the bread.

He liked the dark dripping and would mine it with the end of the knife, carving a tunnel into the marble depths. Her voice was like a silly little dog, he thought, on and on about nothing. None of it was important but like the littlest thorns it was the hardest to remove afterwards from the skin.

'Yes you may leave the table. Bring your book here after half an hour.'

He hated that book already. He went out of the room, past the pantry and through the kitchen, the back way, the way she had told him. The day was to be cut up into separate pieces and her hands would hold the scissors. This piece of the day was to stay in his room.

He opened the door. All the awfulness of the morning rushed out at him.

That was when she had changed from a small kind woman to someone he hated. She had pulled back his bedclothes. In the centre of the sheet was the frog, still wrapped in his handkerchief. Without meaning to, his hand had darted forward, but she had snapped her hand onto his wrist and shaken the handkerchief out over the floor. Startled into liberty the frog had squatted breathing in and out. She had stared at the boy. Her fair skin had begun to glitter with anger, had become spotted with red freckles like the specks in mica or quartz.

She had wheeled around and advanced on the frog.

Her feet were small and hard, clad in polished black laced shoes. He knew how hard the sole of those black shoes would be. The frog's eyes would bulge, the body would become a paste on the carpet. Her feet were small but large enough to be cruel hammers.

Recovering, the frog had leapt away.

Rap, rap went her terrible black feet. The frog jumped under the bed and out again.

Stephen thought he might cry. Once in the street of the town by the river he had seen a dog fighting another dog. There was nothing he could do to stop the smaller dog being bitten; he couldn't enter at all that whirlpool of pain and noise.

'Disgusting, how disgusting,' she kept gasping under her breath.

Another minute and the frog might indeed have been squashed by the mad feet. But then Stephen noticed that only the wire door was shut; the glass door had been latched back to let the room 'air'. He held the door open and by some quirk of fortune the hapless frog hopped away from the blunt feet and out over the step.

She wheeled around and faced him. Stephen wiped the tears away from both eyes with the thumb and finger of one hand, as if he had hardly cried at all. She stared at him and in that moment as her shining black eyes slid over his, he felt something shift between them.

What had he done?

She looked at him for a moment longer and he felt that he had gained something, he didn't know what, by keeping his eyes fixed on hers, by saying nothing. He watched her as she turned away and began to make the bed, pulling the sheets and blankets hard and straight. He saw her hand pause in the middle of the bottom sheet where the frog had been. Then she went on making the bed as though something had happened to her arms and legs, as though something had crawled all over them and left them red and blotched with itching patches. That was the way her face had become when she had been trying to kill the frog.

She finished the bed giving the quilt one last blow.

'You can stay in your room until lunch. Don't think that's the extent of your punishment. I shall allow father to determine that.' Then she was gone, leaving him alone.

Now he walked to the door and looked out through the wire screen at the garden. He couldn't see the frog in the grass. He wondered whether it would find its way back through the uncut stalks and gravel to the ease of the pond. The wire screen pressed against his face in a dense mat. Through each wired boundary he could see if he moved back a little, a tiny square of grass, one filament of a leaf in the hedge, one stone of the gravel. He tried the handle of the door, softly in case she should overhear. It was locked he saw, by a bolt at the top.

He looked back through the wire squares. That was the green of the hedge. He felt the leaves on his fingers, smelt the resin that would remain like perfume. Brown stains would claim you, strong and sticky, and the smell would cling to your hands, bringing the tree with you after you climbed down. The top of a hedge was a street in a different city. You had to force your way in through the brown trunks with their infantry of minor sticks that might rasp or poke an arm or leg. From the gloom of dry stakes, the secret tunnel inside a hedge, you could slowly push your way through to the patches of sky above, forcing your head bluntly against the green. And when you were almost there, for a moment you might shut your eyes as you pushed the last hatch of branches aside. When you opened them again the world of the hedge-top would blind you, the light and space stretch around you like the universe. You could see for twenty miles from the top of a hedge.

Sometimes, without Jessie tagging along, he and Cliff and Joe had climbed half a dozen hedges in a morning in the town by the river. There were days without wind when the hedge lattice clamped its green around you the way the sea swallowed a stone, days when the silence made you whisper and hear secrets, slings and oaths for hours. Huddled like spies in the bristle burrows in the middle of the hedge, a neighbour's passage to the privy could be observed with a nudge of delight. They knew all the hedges of the town, knew which ones were safe, caterpillar varied, and which ones, the best, of a military clipped squareness, were likely to be perilous with sudden shouts by

40

the householder, brooms picked up from beside the tank, cracks on their shoulders as they ran.

On winter days in a high wind they hurried to the hedge before the cold lassoed their legs. You climbed with knee-jerk haste through the lower level. Everything was different, nothing was certain on a day of such wind. Impatient to reach the windy arena above, you just climbed. And on top of the hedge when you emerged, you could see the houses and yards, right before your eyes, in dissolution and decline. Sometimes you might see a line of washing swing and jar, swathe and jolt to the ground, a female calamity. Or you might see apples flung helter-skelter at the teacher.

He thought of pine trees then. Were they best, the wild rush from which all hedges claimed descent, the long unclipped stands of pines that stood to catch the wind and hurry it from the paddocks? Or the blunt draught-horse bulk of a hedge? To keep the winds, to trap it in their topsails, the pines stood on the boundaries of the town, apart yet useful like hill tribesmen who may yet ward off barbarians. They had roamed among these pines, the three boys in the past year.

At the foot of the pines even the earth was different, rank with sheep droppings or the wrinkled hassocks of cowpats, dry with needles and strangely sloped, raised by the bent feet of giants.

You had to select the best tree and begin, knowing that leaving the ground was the hardest part. Once off you could always keep going, up and up, close to the trunk, moving around among the spiral stairs, foot and hand curved on the massive tread, remembered reach and grasp from last year's climb.

They were friends these three and would not mind whether they all climbed one tree or each alone. High in the wind's spaces, feeling their trees pull and rock the earth forty feet below, they would call to each other along the wind-chased boughs, the whole district revealed below as something you could measure between finger and thumb.

Forever after he would associate Mr James and the living-room with the sound of the slow-ticking clock on the mantelpiece.

The long afternoon had come to a close. He had sat for all eternity trying to read and trying to write under Miss Dorothy's eye. It was a grey cold afternoon and the fire in the grate did not warm him. Some bleak foggy air from outside had filled the room. They sat in chairs in the same room all afternoon. Miss Dorothy had also had a book open but she had coughed or talked every few minutes. They had had afternoon tea half way through the afternoon; it had risen in the long dry hours like the oasis of a single tree on a plain. She had set ways of doing everything, even putting down a tray.

And his room? It was nothing more than an alcove, a tent with no door. He would be there alone only for sleep or punishment. He saw a thousand afternoons when he would sit and pretend to read in that low armchair in the living-room, afternoons that would be immeasurable in their boredom, hours when his legs and arms would crawl with impatience and cold.

From his room he had heard Mr James come in and now he waited, sitting on the edge of the bed.

He opened the door of the living-room.

Mr James stood in front of the fire with his hands behind his back. He could pull you forward with his eyes and so Stephen walked straight across the room to him and stopped on the other side of the rug while the eyes looked at him in silence.

'What were you doing in my room?' Mr James asked suddenly turning away to poke at the fire.

He had not expected to be asked that.

'Nothing,' he stammered. In fact he had forgotten that he had even been there. There was a silence.

'But you were there? We found mud on the carpet.'

'Only for a moment.'

'Only for a moment.' Mr James looked down at him.

It was then that he noticed the clock on the mantelpiece. It had a white face and numbers he couldn't read, strokes like letters, not the homely one to twelve that he was used to. It stood in a little black house with columns on either side of the face.

'I don't believe you. You were there for a reason. It's bad enough that you think you have the right to pry into every corner of our house. But you compound your other faults by lying.'

Stephen felt his face burn. He could think of nothing to say. What would be the right thing to say? That face had decided about him yesterday and now it would just watch him in silence, watch his face, move right inside his head until it knocked against the bones at the back of his neck. In the silence he heard the clock tick and then after an infinite time tick again.

'You had better own up,' Mr James said quietly.

Stephen stared at the fire. Once when he had been playing on the edge of the river he had stepped backwards into a hole. Cliff had grabbed his shirt as it floated upwards. They had laughed about it later. He had dried off in the heat of summer. He could never tell the other two any of it. The water had filled his eyes and nose and mouth, burning completely and he was as helpless as a scrap of paper in the flames. There was no descent, no travelling, it was drowning begun in an instant, without hope.

'I was just exploring,' he said, knowing in his own voice the clear note of innocence and realizing it would not be heard.

'No you weren't. I think you'd better own up.' In the silence he heard the clock's slow ticking. It could have been a praying mantis walking forward with giant round all-seeing eyes, step, step, step, with mechanical tread towards the inconsequence of a moth. He saw the hard black eyes and the extreme delicacy of the long legs advancing, the tabby-grey softness of the moth, slowed by the daylight, blinded by the cold. Tick, tick, tick, there was a litany in the artistic hestitation of those waving claws, in that slow approach of death.

'You're lying. You're a liar. I shall have to tell the school this, you know, when I take you next week.'

Mr James turned away to the fire and then swung back.

'But I expected as much. From you.'

There was nowhere now. The eyes reached to the back of his head so that he couldn't remember whether he was naughty or not, couldn't find, within, the smallest space that was his own; like the moth realized that step, step, step, meant claws, darkness, now.

Jessie sat in the covered coach as it slowly climbed the hill.

Inside she felt the same breath and tongue but outside she seemed to be a different person. She had been washed. Up and down the small legs and arms the soap held in unfamiliar hands had pushed its way. Then, worse, her hair had been washed so that her eyes burned, and then her old clothes, now without her body, a mere crumpled heap in the corner, had been left on the floor and she had been dressed in a strange new set of knickers and camisole, stiff socks and soft shining shoes. Over all, she had had a new dress put on her. It was very long. Her knees were hidden. When she had pulled back the dress to see the knees the hands that had washed her had moved in quickly and pulled down the dress so that the knees were hidden again. Now the unfamiliar hands were folded in the lap of the round woman in the black skirt who sat next to her on the jolting seat. When Jessie sat on the shiny black seat, the newly covered knees, belonging as they did to legs too short to reach over the edge of the seat, shot straight out in front on the black seat.

'Are you cold Jessie?'

The strange woman had a gentle face. She had been silent most of the way, but now she had been kind in her tone. Jessie thought for a moment. 'No, I am not cold,' she announced finally.

They were travelling slowly. The hills were too low to be called mountains but they were very steep and the horses were straining. Outside the window the trees which were of a robust sturdy type, not like the mallee near the town on the river, were flashing and glinting. Lights raced this way and that along the grass and sometimes slid through the blue air from tree to tree in the early morning shadows.

What was an aunt? The strange woman, Mrs Whaite, was one it seemed. She had disturbed the peace of the little cottage while it was dark and ignoring the father had assumed control, like some strange version of a mother, reaching out long arms to snatch belongings from where they lay about the room and pack them quietly into one large angry bag, sitting squat and hungry on the ragged bedclothes. Then there had been breakfast, a strained embarrassed episode with father seeming huge and clumsy trying to offer breakfast and finally unsuccessful in all his offers, sitting down near the fire and eating a slice of hard bread and dripping. Jessie found it hard to eat the bread and milk that Mrs Whaite placed before her. Most strange of all, when she endeavoured to eat she found one hand constantly removed from the bowl and placed again in her lap. But eventually the strange meal was finished and Mrs Whaite took the large bag in one hand and her hat in the other and walked onto the front step, father shambling behind.

It was very early. The little town lay like a sleeper just awakened. The sun had crept into the wide dusty streets but it hadn't warmed the buildings. Dark shadows stretched out from walls. A man moved slowly down a nearby street coughing; in the silence the sound barked. The buildings looked sedate and imposing in the early morning sun; without the disorganized scale of human activity in the streets they could suppose themselves for a minute on the edge of a strange and imposing town, instead of one they knew.

'Well Mr Sheldon, Jessie and I had better be getting along. Doesn't do to prolong these things. Now Jessie, say goodbye to your father.'

Father fumbled his hands around her neck.

'Little girl, little girl.'

'I want to say goodbye to Stephen.'

'But dear,' Mrs Whaite looked at Mr Sheldon, 'Stephen's left already to live with his uncle.'

Jessie laughed.

'I'm getting all mixed up.' She spun around in the new dress. Mrs Whaite smiled, embarrassed.

'His chance.' Father said suddenly. 'His chance.'

He stood there looking hopelessly around him. Jessie stopped. How to say goodbye to a father and a town; all one's time and days; for a four-year-old the whole circle of life. Jessie felt a great silence around her. She knew something was happening but she couldn't think quite what it was. She stood there twisting the strange new dress. Father looked foolish, equally unable to speak. He bent his shabby head and kissed Jessie's upturned anxious face. He was angry despite himself. They stood there awkwardly.

Mrs Whaite controlled the situation.

'Goodbye then, Mr Sheldon.' She beat back what she felt at the parting of father and daughter. To regularize the emotion she felt she held out her gloved hand to the large shambling man. It was duty. She reminded herself that Charlie Sheldon was an unsuitable father, he drank and was in and out of work. The mother had deserted the family. It was no place for the four-year-old girl and her brother. Despite these excellent reasons she felt the child's fear and the man's regret striking against her face. I didn't know who was the most upset she would tell her husband, that night in the safe dark of their bed, his arms.

Then she had taken the girl and walked away and boarded the coach that was to take them to the city. The child waved from the window as if she didn't understand anything.

'Everyone to descend please!'

Jessie stared out of the window of the coach; the monotonous hills and trees stopped jumbling past. Everyone looked around. The driver shouted out again and people started to stand up.

'Come on Jessie, we have to walk. The hill is too steep for the horses.' Mrs Whaite was stepping out of the coach into the cold morning. She turned and put her stout arms under Jessie's arms and swung the strange little figure like a doll down onto the ground. They began to walk up the hill. Even though it was early morning Mrs Whaite soon had to wipe her face with a handkerchief. They began to lag behind the knot of other passengers. Further back the horses were straining, their massive legs and chests bulging with the effort to drag the coach up the hill.

The passengers reached the top of the hill. It was a day in early June and the sloping hills dotted about with their thick handsome gum trees looked neat and benign. They waited on the crest. In a few minutes the woman and child joined them and turned with them to watch the coach slowly pulling itself up and up. Jessie stared at the horses. She was hot. Legs and skirts that were unknown to her moved about talking and she was lost in the flow of words and events. If only she could take off the dress and shoes, then she felt that she would be seen and acknowledged. She felt stares. Stares at her dress and her hair. Her legs prickled. She felt she ought to ask the lady something but she didn't know what it was. Which question could she ask first?

Then the huge coach arrived and they climbed inside again. In a minute it set off, the horses relieved at the downhill slope, setting a fast pace. The jolting lulled her and she fell asleep against Mrs Whaite's arm so that all the faces and eyes could no longer see her, and all the questions were left unasked and unanswered.

When she awoke, for a horrible moment she didn't remember where she was. Then she recalled the morning's events. It seemed months ago. She gazed out of the window of the coach, hot and stupid from sleep. They were on a crest, and there, larger than she had dreamt, lay the city. Hundreds of houses stretched out in neat lines to the hills that curved around the city like a protective arm. They seemed in some places about to creep down amongst the houses by sending out winding lengths of trees that, clustered together, almost hid the houses. The roofs were mostly tin, their greens and reds forming a patchwork in the morning air. Here and there was a verandah painted in vivid yellow and green bands of colour. From nearly every roof a thin thread of smoke arose and drifted silently upwards, presently disappearing into the sky.

For the first time staring at the city she found the thought of Stephen. He had been pushed to the back of her head but now he suddenly slid in front of her eyes painfully and terribly. All the things she had been so careful not to think about came flooding back. Miss Dorothy. Herself, staring at him in his new clothes, his soft arms around her neck, her tears. He had understood. She had not, and had danced away from his farewells. Their world was one where exits and entrances were made with a casual air. Just as the shadowy figures of mother and father had always disappeared and re-emerged without cause or explanation so she had assumed would Stephen. She had barely noticed his going. But as the days passed she had become bored and confused in the little house by herself. And one morning standing by the wall of the house, she had picked up a stick and run it along the stones so that falling into crevices, it had made a sharp clicking sound. With every jarring noise a shudder ran up her arm and every blow, there, there, there, seemed to thrust at her the thought that he would not be coming back.

The city wavered. Smoke suddenly drifted sideways and the patchwork of roof colours became mixed. The pain burnt out through her throat and eyes and came out as a sob, a rain of silver tears.

'Poor thing, she's tired,' Mrs Whaite explained to the other passengers.

They stopped at a house. A woman came out of the house hastily undoing her apron and carrying it in one hand. She smiled uncertainly.

Jessie followed Mrs Whaite through the front gate. It dragged on the ground. A face was staring at her through the front window.

'What a journey, we've had, Bertha!' She held out her hand to Jessie, 'And this is our new little girl. Shy I'm afraid but I'm sure we know the remedy for that.'

Suddenly a pair of large arms encircled Jessie. Her face was dusted with kisses. Then just as suddenly she was free again as though nothing had happened. Bertha looked at her, beaming.

'I've brought her things – such as was worth bringing.' The cab-man brought in a large box and placed it on the front verandah. The face at the window looked down at the box, then disappeared.

Jessie had never seen the box before. How was it hers? What did it contain? Her feet wanted to run over to the box but her legs would not move.

The woman who had kissed Jessie was talking to Mrs Whaite in a quiet voice. Jessie had ceased to listen. She was standing on a narrow path of rolled gravel. Large sharp stones bordered the gravel and she looked at them, afraid for a minute that she might fall. White and red roses grew in the centre of the neat garden beds and their scent mingled with the smell of the white and honey coloured freesias that crowded between the bed's rock border.

Inside the house it was warm and noisy. They walked down the central hall of the house into the kitchen. Jessie saw a face peep at her from inside one of the doors. They were in a line, Mrs Whaite in front, Bertha behind, herself last. She stopped. The face reappeared from behind the door and a hand shot out. Then a leg appeared and finally half a child appeared. Jessie stared. The child, a girl, was about the same size as she was.

Mrs Whaite took Jessie by the hand, 'Come into the kitchen dear. You can meet Bessie and Frank later.' Jessie suddenly found herself sitting high up on a comfortable lap. Bertha sat opposite.

'Don't mind the mess; expected you later,' Jessie heard from behind her head. 'No, no.' They talked together.

Outside rain began to clatter on the back verandah. The kitchen had grown dark.

Then the face that Jessie had seen earlier appeared in the kitchen doorway followed by a taller boy. Introductions were made and the names Bessie and Frank descended from somewhere in the air like souls, hovered above the two pink fair children and settled upon them irrevocably so that they could be no other.

The three children were given scones. Jessie was placed on the floor.

'Is she sleeping in our house?' It was the girl, Bessie.

'Yes, dear.'

The boy was looking at his scone 'I've got raisins,' he announced solemnly. 'They all have raisins,' the mother said calmly. The three children began to pick out the raisins from the scone.

'Don't do that. Just eat properly please.' They began to eat like model children. And then they began to gobble like ordinary children.

'Go away and play you two. Show Jessie where your dolls are, Bessie.' The little girls stared doubtfully at one another.

'She's not having my trolley.'

'Frank! Now play nicely. I don't want to hear anyone squabbling.' Mrs Whaite sighed and began to talk to her sister. Bertha had watched the whole scene, allowing herself to smile a little; they were very close, the sisters, and lived only four doors apart.

In Bessie's bedroom there were dolls and Bessie's wooden blocks. Frank sat in a corner pushing his trolley around one leg of the bed. The trolley was loaded with tins. There were dolls' clothes everywhere. There were pencils and small horses and strange pieces of wood and little soldiers.

Jessie was dressing a doll called Martha. Bessie, the same age, could dress and undress her dolls so quickly that Jessie could only watch with puzzled envy. Dolls seemed all legs and arms to her. They were new and wonderful. She loved Martha. But suddenly Martha slipped and one of her small hard hands dug into Jessie's leg. Martha fell head first onto the linoleum. Her eyes clicked shut.

'You've killed her,' Bessie turned with concern for the half-dressed victim.

51

'She's silly,' Jessie retorted. Martha spread-eagled and inelegant was snatched away and a doll called Anne was taken out of the doll's cradle and Martha put to recover, blankets up to her china chin.

Outside the window the June squalls swept back and forth refusing to let the curtain of clouds go up long enough to reveal the temperamental sun. Rain beat upon the bleak window, rattling the pane.

The two girls slept together in a room next to the mother and father. The mother would come in when they were both in bed. She would go over to Bessie and lean over so that Bessie was hidden by her shoulder and head. Good-night Mummy. Good-night. Then she would come over to Jessie's bed and put her lips to the girl's small cheek. Jessie loved that moment. Mrs Whaite always smelt like scones or roasts or soap, the brown translucent soap that they used when they had a bath, not the yellow flat soap that they used for washing. She smelt like the house, shabby and comfortable. Then she would switch out the light and go out leaving the door ajar so that her figure would be silhouetted against the dim light from the hall.

The room was very dark. After a while they could see vague shapes, each others' beds and the wardrobe. The house was very quiet. Sometimes the baby awoke in his room next door and his cries would break out upon the air, the noise floating in the dark.

'My mother's pretty.'

'My mother's pretty.'

'Your mother's – your mother's dead.' Bessie stopped, aware that she was wrong but not knowing any other appropriate category in which to put an absent mother.

'She's not!' Jessie said angrily.

'Well, where is she?' There was silence. A large blue hat floated into Jessie's mind. Was mother dead, like Martha on the floor, her clothes half off? She had forgotten about mother and her words had been, until challenged, just mimicry. Now she thought of the house, of father and of mother. She didn't think of Stephen. She saw the memory of him in the distance out of the corner of her eye but she carefully turned away from that pain. Bessie, she saw, was asleep, her thumb in her mouth in the darkened room.

Jessie was walking to the wharf with Stephen. She saw his longer legs in front of hers. She saw his familiar back and arms. They were going the way they always did over the grassy rise. The river spread out in front of them like rippled glass. But she stopped. Her legs were glued to the ground. She grew into the ground like a tree. Stephen kept on walking. Words would not come. She couldn't shout and a terrible weight held her limbs. Suddenly a wind came up and picked Stephen up like a feather blowing him into the sky until he was no more than a mote, a speck. Hot tears ran down Jessie's cheeks. She was in darkness, at the bottom of a mine of sleep, entombed in the dream.

A light went on. The figure of the mother appeared in the door and came over to the bed.

'Don't cry, dear; don't cry it's only a silly old dream.'

The mine sprang back but Jessie's heart ached. The tears ran down the wet cheeks. 'Stephen,' she sobbed.

Mrs Whaite started. 'Just go to sleep dear,' she soothed, 'Don't cry. Now come on, there's a good girl.'

Jessie blinked. Stephen vanished as though he had never been beside her, never walked across the wharf with her through the enchanted air.

4

Life became a cycle of events. Some giant wheel turned perfectly every day, rolling before it all the inevitable meals and sleeps and baths and long sleeps, so that one followed the other and she was caught up in the turning of the wheel and deposited before the table or in the bath or in bed without having time to think. So that after months and days of all these events she began to know what each event would be like although she couldn't, still, begin to grasp which event followed which, could never determine whether it was to be afternoon or morning tea, couldn't end her activities in time for any event.

A warm plump arm might enclose her and seat her on soft knees and Jessie would twist from side to side, half hating the clean face that she knew was the result of her captivity and yet half loving the soft face that the clean face was, at last, allowed to kiss. This was something really new – having so much of the time a large face regarding her. The world had been one where the sides of necks or the curve of cheeks had been familiar. She had known all the intricacies of her mother's swept-up hair, never felt or played with the combs that held it in place but knew exactly where they mastered the weight of the hair. She knew also the angry streams of tufted hair that fell out from the knot that had, for days, had to suffice as her mother bent over the sewing machine, the children watching the whirring of the treadle from the nest of their bed. She had known that her father's eyes occasionally darted glances at her, worried and furtive looks that swerved away from her own open brown glance. There were occasions when a strange transformation had overtaken father; these were the times when he would appear in the house with wet black hair falling straight from a white line down the centre of his head, and this strange hair would complete a face as smooth as the white of his shirt. Then he would gaze at Jessie, sometimes even take her by the hand and walk with her through the streets of the little town to the river.

But Jessie had never known a large face to appear so often before her. She knew that the face turned this way and that: to the baby, hot and wet in his cot or to Bessie unable to push her fork into her meat, or even to the father who left before breakfast and always came back for tea; these last glances were different.

But increasingly the face swerved to hers. It might be in the bath when she sat playing with the soap and boats, enjoying the warmth and dangerous intimacy with the mercurial Bessie; the two of them, cut off by the steam and isolation of the bathroom, taking strange voyages in a claw-footed boat. Then the face would look at her and smile as it suddenly appeared with towels and drained the water away.

There were lots of meals eaten together around the kitchen table. Mrs Whaite sat at the table with the children but one arm was occupied with the baby, Albert, in his high-chair. After a while, Jessie saw that the baby grew from this arm, extending like a flower from the hand that constantly tipped food from the spoon into his delicate mouth, or offered him a crust, or wiped milk away from his reddened chin.

While one arm thus belonged to the baby, the other hand could pour milk for Jessie, or spoon out more custard or take the fork from one hand and put it into Jessie's other hand;

this happened several times during each meal and Jessie was always amazed since she could not understand how the fork travelled mysteriously into the other hand. Certainly the fork fitted more easily into one hand: from this hand it was constantly taken. Always when the fork was taken, Jessie discovered that the face looked straight at her, large, not cross, waiting; so that sometimes, eye to eye, knowing her own smallness, connected, accepting her own powerlessness and yet silent afresh, with the wonder of her own existence, she felt she might fall into the eyes of the mother's face, and wondered if this was the whole of life.

Outside the back door, off the verandah, a gravel path led straight down the garden and there were fruit trees, vegetables, order. But in the space of the children's days, the garden was not, at all, a straight path and the flowering, fruiting and colouring of the Alberta peaches, the apricot and sullen fig. Nor was it the rows of vegetables between the tank and the fence or the collection of eggs after the mid-morning shrieks of laying triumph had died. For the children the garden did not function, it simply was there, constant, immense and immeasurable. Bessie and Frank ran through it, careless of the boundaries between its experiences; for Jessie it was a world of events.

It was easy to detach herself from the other children who hung around the bustling heat of the laundry. Mrs Whaite's sister Bertha had appeared in the steam of Monday morning as she always did. The two women worked all day around the copper and tubs.

Jessie walked away down the gravel, her steps quickening to a run so that her old dress and pinafore flew out around her knees. The steam and conversation of the laundry receded into the distance and the hot still freshness of the morning fell like a wall of sun between Jessie and the house. Squatting to watch the meandering hens, she looked back at the little figures of Mrs Whaite and her sister outside the laundry. In interminable rhythms of washing and rubbing and conversation, leaning against the laundry wall, carelessly rubbing their wet arms on their aprons, they talked in long stretches of report and dissection, watching the movements of eye and eyebrow, talking, work as serious as the slowly turning world of boiling sheets.

While the labour of washing renewed the physical comforts of the daily existence of two families – made in fact, their very existence into something more than unease and scarcity – so the conversation was full of seriousness, humour and intent: it ranged across the full worlds of their lives and brought the fleece of circumstance spinning into the thread of purpose.

In the silence of the end of the garden, the hens rushed to Jessie. The floor of the fowl-house was raised above the level of the garden so that the hens' heads were level with Jessie's own. She knew each hen felt itself to be different. Now they clustered at the side of the cage, their scaly feet clasping the mud, never stopping defining and redefining their inch of dirt. The caws and murmurs and shrieks they made pulling at the grass her fingers managed to push through the wire were orchestrated by the rooster, a strutting king with a trembling red crown.

The hens rushed backwards and forwards behind the cold net, blundering after her in a futile, impossible rush to escape the aridness of their rich-smelling yard. The chooks were let out late in the afternoons, tumbling into freedom and scattering into the garden to peck small distant snail Americas. But in the mornings they would restlessly peck at her scrappy ration of grass. She loved best to dream and gaze at their world, in recognition of the timber-edged space of their yard, the distant mess of their water, the range of hills, grey and white beneath the perch and the soft mysteries of the laying boxes. Their lives, all the importance of squabbles, of pushes, the fluttering tyranny of the rooster, were carried out between the caged walls of tin, in this one space of trodden earth.

The evening was the time when the house could become unfamiliar; the time when the world which was full of marvels, of certainties and patterns filled with dark, with uncertain space. The day ended peaceably enough with the usual bickering among the long stretches of sun between the fruit trees, precipitating the bath for Bessie and Jessie. Bath time was a gust of activity down the hall of the house that the baby watched with the passiveness of one already fed and only shortly awoken.

In the water Jessie marvelled: I'm the same as Bessie. They sat opposite after Mrs Whaite had briskly washed them both, allowed to play. Down there where the soap or the face-washer might be made sometimes to drift, was a parting, a cleft that made their round bodies in the hot water seem as though they mirrored each other. Or were fruit from the same familiar tree. The boy, Frank, had a funny little bunch. It was very strange.

After Mrs Whaite disappeared from the bathroom, there was, as there often was, a shuffling outside in the hall and the baby slowly crawled across the hard red floor of the bathroom and stared at the girls in the bath, his plump spreading fingers holding the edge, his face alight with food and curiosity, his square bulk emphasized by the home-made knickerbockers assembled by the long labour of Mrs Whaite's hands.

'Warer, warer.'

He bounced and shouted, informing the girls. His fat hands grabbed for the soap, for the face-washer. Perhaps he would fall in, head first. Would a baby float or would he drift to the bottom and soften on the outside to a pulp like the soap? But he dropped down onto his bottom and crawled in under the bath where there was a damp dank skein of dust and soapy water. Somehow Bessie earned sudden angry looks from Mrs

Whaite, even as she sat warmly content in the water, a storey above the baby, who would be plucked from his lair and carried out.

The bath applied a coat of comfort and heaviness, then nightie and dressing-gown, an ease she had never known. It was followed by supper in the kitchen. A sea of food stretched before her, the heads around the horizon, too tired to talk. Mr Whaite was served and then he and Mrs Whaite talked quickly so that the language rolled unheeded, rain clouds over the forest of the half-dreaming children's heads.

Jessie lay awake to the measure of Bessie's breath, wanting the mother's face again, now, before she could sleep. She rolled onto her stomach and slid her feet out of bed onto the lino and idled down the dark strangeness of the hall to the kitchen.

Another world, such as she had never imagined, appeared in the warm-lit untidy room. Mr Whaite sat at the table in his braces smoking a pipe and reading a paper. There was a teapot and a cake on the table. He was talking about the paper, his teacup in one hand.

'It's a crying shame, a bloke like that.'

'How long have you known him?'

'Years. Seven or eight years. He works as hard as I do an' he's laid-off.'

They stopped as the door opened.

What burst upon Jessie most, as the ribbon of light from around the door spread into the whole square picture of the room, was Mrs Whaite bent over the basin in the sink, washing saucepans. One of her legs was resting bent behind her on a little stool and on one side of the sink was a heap of clean gleaming plates.

She had never imagined that life could go on away from her eyes. She had not imagined Mrs Whaite's existence apart from herself: feeding the baby at meals or washing outside in the laundry, or sitting on the back verandah hiding her eyes over some garment for one of the children.

In the pause before Mr Whaite put down the paper to stare, not unkindly, at the door and Mrs Whaite turned, from long experience wiping her hands, Jessie, anticipating the comfort of that lap and arms, saw that the room was full of work: in the dishes on the sink, in the food on the stove, in the man's cake and the untouched sewing basket that sat on the end of the table. And then in the instant that fell between her eyes taking in the scene and the rapid, unthought-out padding of her feet across the floor, she knew that she had, by coming suddenly into the kitchen, after being long in bed, not only done something unexpected to the two grown-ups but also, by taking the brief comfort of Mrs Whaite's lap, the tickle of that voice in her ear, interrupted something, someone else's solace.

In bed Jessie would lie in the unfamiliar dark, hearing in the distance the sound of the trains, making their way south, only two streets from the house. All these sounds wove about her as she lay curled up in a nest of warmth and sleep and as she drifted away and back into the room, the trams and trains would come and go, as distant and even as the sound of her pulse or the sound she had heard as long as she could remember knowing anything, asleep or awake: the turning and turning of the sea. Dream-borne she would move restlessly in bed, treading the same pattern over and over again until worn-out she sank beneath the surface to some deep.

Then she would awake surprised and forgetful. Bessie always awoke first and Jessie, in some blindness, would hear the small inventive sound of her flat voice as she instructed her dolls from a book on the other side of the room.

Minutes later she would turn, realizing that Jessie's bony brown forehead was silently watching from the edge of the blankets. Breakfast would develop in the same way, Jessie's porridge remaining a flat marsh of milk and sugar as she watched the chopping and scooping of Bessie and Frank, experienced and rowdy, on the other side of the table, only remembering to eat when Mrs Whaite gently pinned back her hair.

The children would be sent out to play one by one after breakfast, Mrs Whaite helping them on with socks and shoes. Jessie would lag behind the other two once they were out on the gravel. Bessie would walk close to Frank and they would play important games. Sometimes they played school, which for Jessie meant long stretches of sitting, whilst Bessie waved a long stick and Frank cowered before her, sitting on a box and writing secretly on an old piece of brown paper. At these times Jessie would watch, by her very presence participating in the games in the hard dust near the tank. Days and months were spent watching and dreaming, half remembering another brother and sister, months when she would smile slowly at their antics and they, knowing she was watching their cleverness, would play even harder and fiercer rites under the heat of the peach tree's shade and the summer-faded blue of the distant sky.

'She's having one of her days'.

Mrs Whaite was sitting at the kitchen table peeling potatoes. Mr Whaite drank his tea unhurriedly. Saturday and the kiddies' shoes to mend.

'Where is she?' he asked putting down his cup.

'She's sitting on the potty in the bathroom, crooning to herself and finding patterns in the floor.'

Watched by her husband, Mrs Whaite put down the potato peeler and the potato into a basin of water, and, as if considering the rhubarb bunched on the end of the table, laid a hand on it.

'I suppose it's not fair to expect everything at once.' Mrs Whaite lowered her voice suddenly; was the child listening? The crooning had stopped.

'Kathleen Reilly still hasn't a clue where Clare went. I saw her at the market last night,' he added. The two families rarely mixed. He hardly knew Clare, his cousin by marriage.

'I think we're stuck with her,' he laughed, knowing how fond she had become of the child, that extra pair of arms around her neck.

'Thank goodness for that.' Mrs Whaite took up another potato.

'How could she leave them!'

'Him.'

'Or him.'

Mr Whaite looked at her face, smiling and wise.

To his wife's next remarks he put his arm round her shoulders, not so much because of the content of her conclusion, which was more or less in the direction that Jessie bloomed when shown love and kindness, but because of the tone and form of the remarks. He loved her for her endless optimism, finding in it not only the freedom to think about serious and depressing things, knowing that she would always be there to act as a spring, an escape out of any mood of melancholia that threatened to overwhelm him, but also because her happiness made him feel a little more worldly, a little more protective of what he would have described to himself (if he had ever had to) as her vulnerability.

Jessie, sitting crossly on the pot, was watching the cracks on the floor, considering the big crack that ran from where she sat to the end of the bath. Feeding into it were dozens of small cracks. It was impossible to see how the big crack could emerge.

The potty was always placed in the same place and she could

see the face and the dog that the cracks made. The faces could be made to move in sympathy with her own face she discovered. Forgetting the voices in the kitchen she began to chant.

'This way and that way and this way and that way.' The words took on a life of their own as they became louder and louder. Mrs Whaite, unwinding herself from her husband's protective arm, could have reflected on the words the child was now shouting, could have dwelt with some degree of pain on any meaning she could divine in the chant but she was not given to mulling things over. It was one of her strong points. She prided herself on decisive action which at this point found particular form in bustling into the bathroom, wiping Jessie's bottom, and pulling up her pants while she carried the potty (with a degree of comfort occasioned only by long familiarity with the task) to the little outhouse.

Mrs Whaite put the parcels in the space under the pram and they crossed the road to the draper's, the children holding hands in a squabbling bunch. Frank and Bessie held open the doors of the draper's and the pram was levered into the shop. Mrs Whaite was consulting a list on a sheet of paper.

'Four yards of calico, please Mr Carr.'

The roll was placed on the counter and the large glinting scissors produced. The draper had hands the colour of sausages. He made a small cut in one side of the roll and then tore the material straight across so that the edge of the cloth curled away from the cut.

'And I'll want some flannel. For Mr Whaite.' The draper's hand wavered between the bolts of cloth.

The children were bored. The two girls wandered a little distance towards the back of the shop. There were two long passages down each side of the shop. Bessie climbed onto a chair that stood in front of the counter and stared at a boy who was sweeping the shop. He worked slowly and carefully, a fat boy in long pants, with flapping feet.

'Called Henry,' whispered Bessie from her seat on the long-legged chair. The girls giggled. The boy turned and looked at them from small eyes. His cheeks were red and fat, his mouth a small hole.

'He's a mongrel,' Bessie confided.

What was a mongrel Jessie wondered and why was Henry one? Would he mind their laughter?

He smiled at them delightedly. Mrs Whaite was calling. They rushed to the front of the shop. The boy stared, his broom forgotten, his hands moving urgently, his large head waving slightly from side to side as the draper, closing the door behind Mrs Whaite, came down the shop to put the broom back into his son's hands.

Jessie, out in the garden under the blinding sun of a summer's early morning, began to creep around the house. She began at the back door and dawdled across to the narrow walkway between the fence and the house, passing under the great umbrella of the peach tree. Carefully walking on the far side of the post that supported a cracked and laden bough, she edged her way around the corner to the vine-tangled path that ran right up the side of the house. The voices of the other children now seemed far-off through the heat; she was conscious of silence and a green-lit tunnel. Tight and comfortable as her stomach felt from breakfast, something in her chest began to spread a cold pain, the ache increasing with every vine leaf she pushed aside. The leaves were scarcely dry, tender fingers of new growth. Jessie could see her hand through the skin of the leaf. To beat her way along the path she broke off some of the sprays of leaves: each crack marked off the pain that mounted as she came to the end of the wall. It was a house with a verandah at the front.

Her feet almost ran around the corner and the space, after the confinement of the side path, burst upon her. The pain her her chest flared up as she saw the emptiness of the verandah. The whole garden suddenly seemed, despite the growing delight of a moment ago, a stupid place. It was like the side path, just a space to walk through to the next corner.

Now she was in the front garden, she could see, beyond it, the empty street. She set off towards the next corner, hope welling up again so that the pain in her chest rose to her throat. The garden was a void despite the bright clutter of flowers and the dense scent of lavender. He might somehow be around the next corner although he had not been around the last. She reached the corner and sprang around it into the cool shade of the gravel. Tears swelled behind her eyes as her feet crunched. No, no one was there, only the quietness of the path and the flower beds all along it. Her heart rose to her throat. In despair she began to walk along the side of the house, kicking her feet.

As she reached the last corner she heard the children talking to their father. A wild unchecked thought sprang up and she rushed around to the back verandah. As the sun leapt onto her face she had time to see the wrong faces of Frank and Bessie as they looked at the father's stitching and see his curious face turn towards her. Her heart broke within her chest and dissolved the morning all round her. She lay in the gravel at the edge of the verandah, oblivious of the father's efforts to calm her, of his voice and arms about her, of the baby's amazement as he balanced on the steps and then began to crumple into tears, uncaring even when Mrs Whaite appeared, called by a half-laughing Frank: oblivious of everything except the pain of Stephen's absence.

Mrs Whaite was retrimming her summer hat. She sat in a low cane chair in the shade of the back verandah with the children playing about on the wood of the verandah or on the steps. School was about to begin for the two girls and Bessie carried everywhere a small case, now depositing it before Jessie, who she knew would be too frightened to touch it. Jessie sat at the foot of Mrs Whaite's chair playing with two embroidery hoops, half watching Frank who was wheeling Albert about in a little old wooden cart. The baby held a stick and was dragging it in the dust. Progress was slow but interesting. Mrs Whaite sighed and then smiled at Jessie. The hat had been bought at Marshall's sale last year; it had not worn well and the straw looked bent and old. But it hadn't been allowed to get wet. It was not split and was now about to be renewed by the replacement of the ribbon. The old ribbon was handed down to Jessie. It left a paler band of straw exposed.

'You can keep the ribbon Jessie,' Mrs Whaite said gently and then seeing that Jessie looked blankly up at her added, 'For your own self.'

Even Bessie had noticed, looking quickly at her mother. Jessie ran the ribbon between her fingers feeling the ribs of the grosgrain. She wondered what colour it was.

Mrs Whaite's face was bent over the hat again as she stitched the new ribbon in place.

School. It was pencil sharpeners and lines and the mat. It was desks and Good-morning Sir to the Headmaster, watched out of the corner of your eye, a dog that might bite.

'One boy in Frank's class got the cane.'

Jessie absorbed that in silence. Mrs Whaite would protect me. Mrs Whaite was a hug, a silent kiss, a pleasure like home when you saw her face waiting outside the school gates and the whole horrid day was over. Jessie walked in the morning with Bessie and Frank but they were in different classes.

'Good-morning, Mrs Brown.'

And then you sat down at your desk and waited. Jessie shared her desk with Ethel Waters who had long plaits and eyes that amazed, looking in two directions at once.

Pencils had to be sharp. The smell was lovely. Sometimes you could hold a thin curl of wood like a flower in your hand all the way back to your desk.

Mrs Brown looked at you through her glasses and then turned around and wrote fast words on the board.

'I'm going to dob on you.'

'Bet you won't.'

'Miss, Miss. Ethel's – .'

'Sit down, *all* of you. Now I'm going to read you a story.'

Then you could dream and look out of the window at the sky while the teacher's voice went on and on and the sky became the sky of the story, blue and far-reaching and you were in the story and all would be well.

They were going to George Road. The baby rode in the pram, Jessie held Mrs Whaite's hand and the other children walked, one on either side, holding onto the metal of the pram, glancing at Jessie from under their hats. They set off down the street towards the tram line in a slow procession. To get everybody dressed and ready in hats and proper clothes had taken hours and hours. Mrs Whaite had rushed between the children's rooms and there had been a moment when, kneeling behind Jessie to do up buttons, she had actually sighed loudly and rushed across to Bessie's clothes for another dress. Then the baby began to cry about the long captivity of the pram and Bessie had had to push him to and fro outside the bedroom door while Mrs Whaite stood in front of the mirror combing her hair and pausing with her hat in hand to tell Bessie not to push so fast, before putting the hat carefully over her hair and taking over the pram, her bag and purse in a final bustle of activity.

But now they were at last walking through the autumn air

towards the shops that lined the road.

When they got to the end of the street, there before them, lay the tramline! Jessie tugged her hand and Mrs Whaite let her go so that she could walk across the tracks by herself. All the children loved that. Frank even put his head down and looked along the silver ribbon of track that glinted in the sun. They walked on to where the shops crowded along the little road. It was a flat suburb and the shops could be seen for a great distance. The sun was low and only the roofs of houses were still a dappled mass of green and brown and shaded chimneys. The two-storeyed shops had gold along their backs; windows which looked down from a great height to mean backyards were eyes of burnished brown that saw for miles and miles over the city. All the shops, it seemed to Jessie, had hats on: they had fancy carved fronts and looked grand, if seen from the street but approached from behind, one saw the façades for what they were, and saw as well the rusting tin of the roof and the untidiness of gables and lean-tos and outhouses.

They turned the corner and walked into the shade of the verandahs that stretched along the footpath. While Mrs Whaite went into the sawdust of the butcher's the children waited outside, clustered around the pram but ignoring the baby who was leaning forward straining the straps that harnessed him to the seat. Next to the butcher's shop was a little tea rooms. The children had never been inside. Through the door could be glimpsed a number of small tables covered with cloths that in the dim light could represent themselves as white, a floor of dark well-used linoleum and a long high counter. A man stood reading a paper in a bored restless sort of way, turning the pages too quickly; no one could read as fast as that. There was never anybody in the shop, just that mysterious darkness. Jessie gazed at the window. The glass was in two panes, divided down the centre by a tall column. Leaves and scrolls decorated its base and burst out again at the top. Behind the glass was a hill of chocolate. At the foot of the glass below her gaze was a mountain range of chocolate pastilles and above them, opened boxes of more chocolates.

'Rowntrees Pastilles and Rowntrees Dessert Pastilles,' Frank slowly told them. Above on the second shelf, almost out of sight, were bowls of round chocolates nestling among dusty potted palms. Why didn't the man eat chocolates slowly all day, wrapping his tongue in that dense taste? In the centre of the window was a metal fan that whirred backwards and forwards, but no matter how long the children watched, it never upset the wavering leaves of the palm.

Time rushed around the year. Christmas delighted the children twice. There were some mornings now when Jessie wandered out into the garden of the house at Goodwood and felt that she had everything, felt that she couldn't want anything more, that this was, indeed, happiness.

The garden renewed itself mysteriously in the night. Next door the small trees were covered with shoots, new leaves, in the morning light, the colour of fire. It was not a suburb with views. That was part of the happiness. The freshness of the morning and the sparkling trees of the garden were one thing.

Something else made her raise her hands to the sides of her face. She knew that inside the house there would be dishes in the sink, beds pulled back to air, the baby in his homely outfits and Mrs Whaite in her work dress and apron, as always, starting the day's events in the right order. She knew too that she somehow fitted into the giant turning of those everyday happenings.

There was a centre that held, that kept the right things happening. She would be fed and clothed and bathed and briefly kissed. She could hear the sounds of comfortable order from the other houses nearby; grates being swept, dishes being washed, clotheslines propped up and babies fed messes in their high-chairs. It was a suburb of housewives.

She was, above all, part of things. She could feel the peace and order of the space around her, the secrecy and contentment of ordinary lives: the peace of Goodwood in autumn 1914, a harmony that in particular, sprang from Mr Whaite reading his journal in a cane chair on the back verandah and from Mrs Whaite laughing with the baby in some room of the house.

As they left the jetty the day's perfection shattered.

The whole day had been marvellous from the moment they left the house in their beach hats and walked down to the train. The ride in the train had been street-flashing ecstasy.

They sat in the front with their bags, four pairs of eyes staring at the trees and houses whirling past. How could mother simply sit, knitting? Soon they came to a long stretch of sandy waste grass, and Bessie, who could remember the last time they went to the beach, told Frank that they would soon be there, and didn't he remember too? There was a final busy rush of tall buildings and trees and then they could see the beach and the sea. Their confusion of belongings was moved out of the train by Mrs Whaite and they set off towards the sand.

Forewarned not to expect any rides or treats from the gay litter of sideshows, the sea became the greatest pleasure for the next hour. Far away from Mrs Whaite and Albert, who sheltered beneath an umbrella back on the sand, the three older children explored and pillaged amongst the debris around the jetty. After the first few moments, they had all wanted to take off their shoes and socks so they could stand, with feet cooled by the waves and stare up at the strange echoing cavern that was the underside of the jetty. It seemed like rock that sometimes echoed to their small voices and sometimes threw down the sounds of unseen children who raced along above their heads. To Frank's grizzle Mrs Whaite agreed. They might walk there.

Up high they felt quite grand. It was a marvellous walk along the vast road of planks that was like a street, thronged with groups of people on the shiny boards, far above the strange depths and suckings of the sea. And then the sudden terror, the terrible panic. Mrs Whaite said, as she rushed the children off the jetty and down the steps to the sand, gabbling the words as the baby might over and over, 'Frank's *missing*.'

The beach a moment ago had been a stretch of pleasures, a magic carpet. Now it was a waste, vast and hostile. Jessie felt a surge of sick as she watched Mrs Whaite flap down to the water's edge. Bessie, who was holding Albert's hand, was only keeping back tears by remaining silent. Mrs Whaite was rushing along the sand shouting thin cries like a gull in the distance.

The sourness in Jessie's throat grew until it seemed as if the sand might suddenly swing sideways and become the sky: the blue of the sky become sea, with that fleece of cloud the edge of the waves, the colours of the day washed away like an illustration on which water had been spilt. But what else caused her heart to thud in her chest behind the tight lawn dress? What hurt more and more when, a few minutes later, Mrs Whaite appeared dragging Frank from the far side of the jetty?

'He had climbed down one of the side steps and waded ashore.' Mrs Whaite was crying.

It had something to do with Bessie's tears as she stumbled off across the burning sand to meet them, falling and almost dropping the baby, and something to do with the shock of seeing not only the cuffed, wet Frank in tears but also wetness on the mother's cheeks.

But more than that, it had to do with Jessie running to meet them, arriving with a sudden twist of pain to find that even though she was crying herself with relief over Frank being found, she had, she knew, greater losses. Most of all it had to do with seeing that even though mother had knelt and put back Jessie's hat and had extended an arm to include her in the group, she was still, she suddenly knew, an outsider.

A long way away, a man died and while his body lay drifting blind-eyed through the muddy water of a shell-hole, so that (in the end) he was not human, just a messed collection of official garments and laced boots that still drifted this way and that to the cataclysms of distant gunfire, while his body lay thus, forgotten in a thundering night, he died more clearly in a certain house, half a world away. His death was not recorded other than a number. He had not had funds to have an elegant serious photograph of himself in uniform taken in a patriotic studio. He was not brave, at least not in a spectacular way, or if he was, it was not recorded. He didn't send home eloquent letters; he wrote awkwardly at regular intervals in pencil. He was liked in the battalion but not popular. He died amongst strangers, ashamedly crying. The usual telegram of regret would be sent.

The women watched from behind curtains as they saw the minister's dark figure approach and pass all the houses: oh pass, oh pass, do not stop with that telegram, carrion news, go on with your news of death: pass.

Mrs Whaite, sitting on Jessie's bed, was reading to the girls before turning out their light. The house was very quiet; Frank and the baby asleep already and no Mr Whaite to step or stir since he had left months ago, dressed in strange hard clothes and a hat with a strap under his chin. Jessie, watching from the warm stillness of her bed, considered the mother without the father. Mrs Whaite became cross more than before. She sometimes shouted. She tore open letters and forgot everything as she read. You could tell that. She supposed this had something to do with what Mrs Whaite and her sister now talked and talked about as they sat sewing on the verandah. He was a long way away. He had gone to fight. Would he fight, that father who laughed and smoked a pipe? Frank boasted at school and other boys boasted too. It was a war. You missed him.

'One more, and then the light's going out,' said Mrs Whaite recrossing her legs. She began to read:

This is the key of the kingdom:
In that kingdom is a city,
In that city is a town,
In that town there is a street,
In that street there winds a lane,
In that lane there is a yard,
In that yard there is a house,
In that house there waits a room,
In that room there is a bed,
On that bed there is a basket,
A basket of flowers.

Flowers in the basket,
Basket on the bed,
Bed in the chamber,
Chamber in the house,
House in the weedy yard,
Yard in the winding lane,
Lane in the broad street,
Street in the high town,
Town in the city,
City in the kingdom:
This is the key of the kingdom.

5

There was, decidedly, nothing worse, Miss Symes reflected, than waiting for someone to arrive. From her verandah she could see the little road that led to the train and she knew from long experience that the train had not yet arrived. Nevertheless she kept on walking along the verandah among the plants and cane chairs, back and forth past the entrance steps. Her walking took her all the way from the door of the dining-room on the west to the door of her bedroom on the east, where, lying in bed in the early morning she could see the tops of the tall saplings tossing the light. Not that she ever lay in bed long. Energy, what a gift she thought, watching the spareness of her shadow and the quick evenness of her stride. Her skirt made a long cone-shaped shadow. She was not dressed elaborately. There was a plainness about her skirt and striped blouse but they were perfectly cut and carefully worn. That and the neat collar and the well-polished shoes would speak for themselves if necessary she told herself.

Along the stone walls of the large house was her pride and joy: pots of ferns and camellias, piled azaleas, lily of the valley, daphne and palms. Some were old specimens, many were in quaint or beautiful pots, all were well-watered and cherished and their careful placing, their profusion and all the delicate touches, like the piece of volcanic rock, here, that nestled between two pots, or the small china pot, just so, in the centre of one of the cane tables, would indicate the leisure and preference of one who lived for beauty.

Not that I'm vain she thought with a laugh. She scorned frivolity in dress. Sometimes she privately reflected that a great many people had, now that the war was on, adopted an attitude in regard to dress that she had long held from motives far more pure and painfully aimed at, than a simple wish to appear patriotic.

It's just sensibility my dear, she thought remembering that she had, that afternoon, before sending Turner and the trap down to Stirling station, paused several times and gone to one of the mirrors in her large drawing-room, mainly, she admitted, to check her hair. Why this nagging sense of not feeling that she knew quite what she looked like? Playing the piano after lunch, she had found herself, on several occasions, sitting silently with her hands still at the keys, the last chord of the sonato echoing only in her ears and the room long since quiet.

It was a very large house and of course sounds from the kitchen would not permeate the front rooms. Sitting at the embroidered piano seat, in the moment before she gave a little start and turned the page to begin another piece, she had been conscious not only of the peace and emptiness of the room with its heavy furniture, polished parquet floor and photographs crowded on the mantelpiece but also, all of a sudden, of a sense of uncertainty about the way the slow ticking of the clock reigned through the stillness from the drawing-room to the dining-room and the passage beyond.

Yes, she thought as she sat with a straight back playing, anyone could guess that she had largely occupied herself with books and literature, not caring a great deal about mastering any of the arts of mere self-decoration. She laboured to perfection through every bar of the sonata. And then she sat. What would the ordered clutter of the great rooms mean to the child? She liked to stroll from room to room feeling the presence of her own and her father's and mother's lives. But she liked to organize as well, she thought, turning in the stillness and moving a photograph a little to the left, an old chair back from the sun an inch or so. Those daffodils! She had forgotten them. She rearranged one of the vases of flowers, culling out the dead blooms and carrying them out to the kitchen.

The same energy that set in motion the tending of the large garden round the house had also ensured that she could now walk on the verandah quite confident that the girl's room was ready, had been readied for some hours with everything that a young girl could require if she were to live not in anything resembling luxury (not even surrounded by the personal mementoes and accumulated ornaments that in her own room she justified in her strict scheme of things by inheritance), but certainly in the utmost of plain comfort. But what was the reason for the little posy of flowers that had been placed on a doily on the child's dressing-table? What was the reason why she paused in front of the mirror in the hall and why, now, she watched with such intent her trap coming up her gravel drive and stopping in front of her great house to let out the woman and the child?

At the big house they walked up steps to a thin woman. It was funny, Jessie thought, that face on such a tall person. It wasn't the face of a grown-up at all.

'Pleased to meet you,' Mrs Whaite began.

The woman was frowning at the air above her head. Leading the way along the verandah, Miss Symes reminded herself there was plenty of time. Theodore had had problems too but they had been overcome. The boy was a credit to him.

'How are you Mrs Whaite? Was the train journey pleasant?'

It's how you talk to children, or I suppose the servants, Mrs

Whaite thought, smiling, holding out her hand. Ought not to have taken off my gloves though.

They had reached chairs and a table set for tea.

'Tea out here. Jessie might like a run.'

A run, as though she was a puppy, Jessie thought.

It was not so much a question as a decision Mrs Whaite mused, looking at Jessie's face. At the table Miss Symes sat down, ringing a little bell as she did so. She turned a bright smile at the child.

Mrs Whaite unpinned her hat and touching Jessie's arm, said, 'Do you want to look at the fish?'

She wouldn't stay here with that woman. Why had they come? She flung her arms around Mrs Whaite's neck and hid her face. But it was no use.

'Dear, dear child.' Mrs Whaite put her arms around her.

Miss Symes bit off the remark she was about to add to Mrs Whaite's murmur and waited. Looking at the hat on the table with its gaudy ribbon she was not surprised, she decided, at displays of temperament. The child allowed herself to sidle away, not taking her eyes off the two grown-ups.

'She's a pretty child, Miss Symes. And good.'

'Stephen's good looking, too.'

'Like their mother.'

'Let us hope not in character!'

There was a silence. And then the tea arrived. Oh how she would cat to Bertha tonight about this spinster's airs.

'Does she always lose her tongue?' Miss Symes asked as they drank their tea. She held out a plate of scones in the direction of the child with another gay smile.

By way of response the child eased further away along the verandah her hands gripping the railing behind her.

Mrs Whaite looked at her feet. Miss Symes would have to be answered. 'She feels everything. But she's not a chatterbox. I've grown very fond of her.'

'Bring everything into the open, that's what I always say. And be truthful – always.'

They fell to talking about the war, 'a subject close to my heart' as Miss Symes put it. Mrs Whaite listened politely, her own heart folded and put away.

Away from the two women on the sunny autumn verandah, across a space of polished wood and lush shrubs the child stood motionless. On the edge of the verandah as they talked on and on, she turned away at last to stare through the leaves and the depths to the ground below.

The father was dead. Tell yourself again and again.

There had been confusions and crying during which Mrs Whaite turned crumpled and red-eyed for days at a time. Jessie had felt things could not be the same. But gradually events began to revolve again and the children became used to a new sort of mother who often sighed instead of talking happily to them as she knelt buttoning up a jacket or pulling on a sock.

Then one morning, a surprise. Jessie found herself being dressed in her best dress, shoes and socks. Nothing could be more alarming than finding her things gone from Bessie's room, so she was not shocked when she ran in to find that Bertha was installed at the table in the kitchen and Mrs Whaite, in her best dress, was ready to go out.

'You'd better tell her.' Bertha got up and tied on an apron.

'I should have before. Things on my mind.'

Letters that were typed and formal and edged in black crowded together along the mantelpiece. Jessie found herself carried to her bedroom. Mrs Whaite knelt before her, then hugged her so that Jessie's heart spun and her eyes closed against the cloth of Mrs Whaite's dress. Why, mother had her hat and coat on. What was going to happen?

'You're going to live in the hills. With a lady.'

The words meant nothing. What had she done?

Jessie looked straight at the mother's face, not listening to the words but gazing, lost in the other's eyes, trying to find some reason there for yet another parting.

'Oh, my dear child. Don't worry. She's a sister-in-law of the man who's been looking after y' brother, Stephen.' Mrs Whaite took Jessie's coat and began to button it.

Even the bald truth, thus presented, was probably too much, Mrs Whaite began to decide, for the child stared at her with wild brown eyes. She hugged the girl again, relieved that she did feel some pain that the brown-haired child would no longer be running in from the garden with her own three, or lying in the dark, another breath on the ocean of sleep, supervised alone until late at night. But the pennies would not cover this child's head and it had seemed a godsend when the answer had come from Mr James.

In the kitchen the two women looked at each other and then at the silent child.

'I can't feel it, Bertha. It seems nothing after Ted, the pain and all of the past few months,' she said to Bertha on her way out to the gate.

Mrs Whaite took Jessie's hand. In her other hand was a large bag.

The other children hung on the gate ready to wave, a line of children. A line of three now, that Mrs Whaite waved back at.

Your brother Stephen. If you skipped and walked even your feet would say the words. That dear face might suddenly slide in front of your eyes the way it had in the house. You said the name over and over.

You might think about him all day and still not see the face, but when someone else said the name the face could suddenly appear. Your brother Stephen like Aladdin's genie in the story. The name had a power but only when someone else said it.

79

The power came from listening to the words. And it was never enough to hear them in your head or say them out loud to yourself when no one else was listening.

Once in the garden of the Whaite's house she had tried that. There on the lawn at the end of the garden by the orange tree was a ring of toadstools. The grass was still wet. She had been dressed early for school and, running out to play, had discovered it. Looked at one way of course it wasn't a ring at all. One side did wobble. But there was no way of knowing. Did the ring have to be perfect? Mrs Whaite's ring was perfect, round and gold and she wore it on the other hand because Mr Whaite was dead. Sometimes she took it off. Frank spun it on its end one night at tea-time and when it fell, he had to crawl under the kitchen table and give it back before he was smacked.

Hesitating in the dew, she had decided that the dirt-coloured buttons did make a ring. And then she had stepped from the lawn into the circle that should have been magic and said the name. Without moving her school shoes an inch she had looked at the garden, the path up to the back verandah, the fruit trees on the right, the chook-house on the left, had searched the garden from where she stood within the circle of power.

Nothing had changed.

Stephen did not appear. The garden was the same garden. The back door had banged and Bessie had called her so that she stepped out of the ring without thinking, tracking into the house dirty toadstools on her good school shoes of all things said Mrs Whaite.

On the way up to this house in the train even the wheels had known the sounds. You could hear them over and over as the engine tugged the carriages up the cuttings. But Mrs Whaite had not heard. She had sat there knitting and telling you to look out of the window, deaf to the music of the wheels.

She looked back along the verandah. The two women had

mentioned the name. So she had not been wrong to think that the train had carried it up here. Here, where she stood on the wide polished verandah she had heard it.

Ah, but now Mrs Whaite was coming towards her with her hat and gloves on to say goodbye.

'I'll answer all your letters dear,' she promised, leaning over and hugging the child. But Jessie ran away. After clinging for one moment to the mother she ran the length of the verandah, determined not to say goodbye.

When you cried the tears ran one after another across your nose and down into the pillow. When you cried for a long time your head lay in a damp patch.

The sheets had been cold and white, like the bluish white of a hard-boiled egg. The woman had given her a kiss on the forehead and shut the door, leaving her to get undressed alone. On the dressing-table she had found a bunch of flowers in a blue vase. Lying in bed she had smelt them through the darkness, a smell like honey, like Mrs Whaite's flowers, like the front garden of that house.

If this were the Whaite house someone would have heard, she thought, heard her crying and come to comfort her. But although she had opened the door when she went across to turn off the light, she knew that no one would hear.

There was a dim light on further down the hall and it made her doorway into a square stage of light, a barrier between darkness and light.

No one else would be left like this. Not Bessie, not Frank, not Albert. And then she had begun to cry. Bessie would be lying asleep. Bessie would be able to hear the sounds of the trains as she herself had done only last night.

But, you, you, were someone who could be left.

You were someone that even a motherly person might be able to turn away from. That made the tears tear and flood out of her throat. Everytime she thought perhaps they would stop, she would think that Mrs Whaite had gone away from her. And then the tears would start again and again, each one bringing back the pain as though she had not thought of it ever before in her whole life, as if she felt it for the first time. You were someone who could be left.

After a long time the tears stopped.

She lay with her cheek on the coldness, staring at the door with swollen eyes, unable to cry or feel any longer.

In caves stalactites hung from the ceiling for thousands of years. They had learnt about them at school. Water dripped down and left sediment. Time after time that happened and where it happened a stalactite grew, hard and cold and yellow, sealing its length with thousands of years of silent damp. Lying with her head on the pillow, unable, after so many tears, to cry any more, she looked out into the dimly lit passage and felt a dull sort of peace. That pain she felt was sealed off by her tears; each fresh wave of tears had grown a sediment and there remained now as she drifted into sleep, a strange shape, as strong as stone.

When they set off next morning for the school, the air met their faces like a cold blade.

It was about a mile, a lovely walk Miss Symes said. Such views! She had special heavy boots on. She walked with a bounding step as they set off on the winding track.

Jessie felt she knew already that Miss Symes would not be unkind. After breakfast when she had gone to get her hat, to her surprise she saw that it had a new ribbon. This ribbon was navy blue. The old ribbon was red.

'Where's the red ribbon?' she asked as they stood on the front verandah about to leave. She held out the hat to Miss Symes. She would not put it on till she knew. The red ribbon had been sewn on by Mrs Whaite. The red ribbon went around the crown in a circle of gaiety and recall. Mrs Whaite had sewn it on in the kitchen of the house in Goodwood. Afterwards Jessie had gone to stand in front of the mirror, liking the girl who looked at her in a hat with a red ribbon.

Miss Symes carefully shut the wire door and took the hat.

'Navy is much more suitable, Jessie. You're growing up remember.' There was a silence.

'I think you'll find nearly all the girls at the school here have navy.' The child twitched the hat away but did not put it on.

'However, you can certainly keep the red ribbon. We can put it on another hat.'

It was a truce. All she had wanted was to prevent the child looking cheap. Red was vulgar.

She watched with relief as Jessie put on the hat.

'I'll put the ribbon on your dressing-table,' she promised as they set off. It would be a pity to let anything spoil the beauty of such a morning.

When they saw the school Jessie felt very brave. It was much smaller than the school at Goodwood. It stood alone in a paddock, fenced off from the bush all around, a small squat building of grey stone. They were late and from inside the school there already came a low hum. But it could not contain many children she thought.

Miss Symes stood on the steps talking to the teacher. Inside Jessie could hear the monitor talking in a loud voice to the children. Then Miss Symes left.

'Come in, then Jessica, and I'll perform the introductions.'

Standing in front of the whole school she felt herself go red. How could she have thought there would not be many children?

The boys, well perhaps they did not matter, but there seemed to be hundreds of pairs of eyes above plaits and pinafores that looked at her. She found herself seated at a large table with a great many other girls and boys. Everyone stared. Only one girl smiled. Jessie was given an exercise book on which the teacher wrote Jessica Sheldon in large capitals. On the front cover of the exercise book was an arch of leaves over an emu and a kangaroo who between them held a badge, a giant badge propped casually against their attendant feathers and fur.

At playtime the girls all sat under the trees on benches eating their lunch. Jessie's hand went down to her sandwich and back again. And each time it was as though she had on a glove. Other girls were watching her from the end of the bench. It seemed to take an age to eat and her hand would move in such a heavy way.

All the girls went away and began to skip when they had finished. There was nothing she loved as much!

She finished her sandwiches at last and folded the papers and put them back in her case. And still no one asked her to join in. She sat for a moment longer. She would ask herself!

She walked over to the line of girls, each step a fall further into the pounding of her heart. No one looked at her but she knew they had all noticed her coming. The rope went on and on, cracking the ground and still no one spoke.

When the last girl was out there was a silence.

'Can I go next?' Jessie shouted, hearing a strange new voice.

'You can turn,' said a tall girl. And she handed Jessie her end of the rope.

She was in! The rope went down into the dust and up again, round and round, lower than your feet and higher than the highest trees, carving for you, as you stood turning and turning, an arc of sky and sun.

She made friends.

But school remained school. There was something about it, something she did not understand. Something happened at the school gates. Something that, no matter how many times she thought about it, she still could not understand. It had happened the second time she had been taken to the school by Miss Symes. One minute they had been outside the school, outside the little picket fence. The next instant they were inside, being stared at by everyone. The girls darted away to form into whispering groups near the fence.

After a while, the strangeness of school began to wear off. But the power of the school fence to change things did not diminish. The children were not allowed out of the grounds all day. There was enough space for the girls to sit on one side and boys the other, even enough space for separate gangs of girls to sit and plot under the pine trees so that when lunch was over, a sudden explosion of girls might advance upon another group, taunting and calling. But it was as though the fence could not contain the energies of the children: new forms and rules might appear in the strange alchemy of the school grounds. Outside the gate, child might tease child, but there was the air and the light blue fragrance of the bush all around to diffuse malice, but once a child stepped in past the heavy gate, heard the click of the latch behind, then by some strange process everything and everyone was different. Friends might become enemies, sisters might be ignored or brothers taunted. And so you learnt, like all the others, to watch, to harden and to be prepared for the sudden call from the girls turning the long skipping-rope or the cold stare from the girl wheeling away, arms linked with another, the secrets and lent pencils of the day before now all forgotten.

All her days fell into a path that led to just one day. School for five days, Saturday, and church on Sunday. Next month Stephen would come to visit. She couldn't understand why it had to be next month and not this month. Miss Symes had told her just to be patient. That was not a reason.

She thought about him every day. Each night she crossed

off another day. Seven days made a row, a line of days that you could run the pencil down. Sometimes she would run her pencil half way through the next day to see if it made any difference. It felt dangerous. It made the day last longer she decided in the end.

She thought about Stephen and all the days until he should come every night, like a prayer, as she got into the bath. The bathroom, at the end of one wing of the empty house, echoed to the sound of her bottom and legs subsiding under the water. The sound of the chip heater ran like a waving hand's shadow all around the white tiled walls and then died away. She waited till the water was as perfect a line as the row of red tiles that bordered the walls. She sat motionless in the warm water watching her legs turn pink. She would see tiny ripples flow out and cling to the chain that dropped down into the water and dribbled towards the plug; she would see one side of the bath see-saw into balance with the other side. At long last there would be silence, the water would sleep around her feet. Then she would feel how long it had taken, how long it all took. Already the water would be cooling. She would want to slide down and warm her shoulders. Miss Symes would knock at the door and tell her to have a good wash and please get out.

And when she climbed out it would be bed-time and a fraction of time, no more, would have passed. Only when she looked back at the days and weeks that she had been able to run her pencil through could she see that time was not standing still.

Suddenly, one day, there was only a week to go.

Then it was the day after tomorrow, then tomorrow.

And then it was today, a sunny August Saturday but the morning had to be endured, a time when she felt the sun might have stopped so slowly did it move around the house.

A strange face, an old man, stared at her when she ran in to the sitting-room after lunch. Miss Symes in her small chair smiled a little. The great room contained only those two. It was dusty empty space.

'There's someone you won't remember outside.'

It couldn't be true. That man was too old to be Stephen's guardian. Let them drink tea by the window. She would go to the kitchen and ask Mrs Turner, the cook, for some cake.

'Don't go away so rudely. This is Mr James.'

And so she must advance and shake hands, while her heart burned and her feet itched. What a silly pair they were.

'Well then, off you go,' the old man said abruptly as if she were wasting his time. She circled to the door.

Stephen would not be there. It was impossible to believe after such a long time. In the garden they had said. She went out into the huge expanse of lawn and shrubs. The garden! It stretched for ever. He might be anywhere. She began to look without hope in the shrubbery at the front where the shadows stretched bleak and cold, long into the late winter's day. Then she looked around the side garden, turning back to the house with a sense of having been the butt of a cruel joke by the grown-ups.

'Jess.'

She turned slowly. There, having stepped out from behind a hedge, he stood, unsmiling, taller and older, not the boy she knew or remembered, but nonetheless Stephen.

She couldn't move in case he vanished, couldn't speak for the joy that rose in her throat so in the end he had to walk down the path towards her, while the world trembled, her double vision of things wrestled to cede into one final whole, and with the pain that came with his touch on her shoulders, his hug, his voice, she knew that with the knowledge they now had, they could never be so parted again.

After that they played hide and seek as if they had never been separated, as if they lived together and could be careless about each other. Jessie ran shouting through the garden when it was her turn to hunt. When it was her turn to hide she hid where Stephen would find her quickly.

For in her heart she hadn't wanted to play hide and seek at all. It had been Stephen's idea, not hers. What had she wanted to do? She didn't know but it wasn't this terrifying losing and finding.

The trees stretched their shadows longer and longer across the gravel. Her feet crunched as she ran. She hid behind the jacaranda tree. The trunk was cool against her hot cheek. If she moved her head a fraction she could see Stephen, running, looking for her with a frown. Of course he found her easily. She didn't know if she liked that, the way he scorned her hiding places. The jacaranda tree was a favourite anyway; it was worth hiding near it just to smell the bark, to put your arms around its trunk and hear, after all that running, the sound of your heart sinking into the wood.

'My turn. Count to a hundred this time.'

A hundred, not forty. How long that took! Before she reached thirty the sound of his feet died away to nothing. At seventy she heard the garden rustling as though it had covered him under a season's leaves. Opening her eyes at last, the garden looked too bright to absorb, too bright to search. She set off. She looked in the shrubbery and in the hedge that screened the side garden. Then she ran downhill all the way to the gates. She spent a long time peering under the hedge near the gates. But he wasn't there. She set off back to the house. While her eyes had been shut, she saw that the whole garden had changed. It was nearly dark now. Where were the grown-ups? Where was he?

She couldn't search the garden in that darkness. Two lights went on in the house as she walked up the steps. She went along the verandah, without any hope of finding him, around the corner and along the side. At the end of the verandah, stone steps led down to a cellar. And there she saw him.

He was crouched on the bottom step, looking up at her so that she saw his face after he'd seen hers. He wasn't smiling until she did and she saw his face was different. In the cold of a winter's dusk, every feature looked back at her as though through flames, everything she'd known shimmered back, dissolved as if burnt by a wall of heat.

Then it vanished.

She shouted down trying to sound happy, 'Why'd you hide there? That's the sort of place where you'd never ever be found. Like a grave.'

He came up the stairs, smiling. Her heart raced.

'I know. Let's go in and have tea,' was all he said. And she laughed because he had.

One morning Miss Symes, refreshed from a long night's sleep, began to teach Jessie the piano.

'It isn't going to be easy. The child seems to have no concentration,' she remarked to Mrs Turner.

She came to the kitchen for milk at 11 a.m. Miss Symes believed there should be no nonsense about servants especially these days. She often came and helped herself and carried her own tray out for morning tea. The cook turned away from the stove. A high narrow window illuminated the kitchen and through it Charlotte Symes suddenly noticed the sunlit trees on the slope behind the house.

'Look at those trees, galloping through the wind's paces in a mass of green and blue. Look, Mrs Turner aren't they beautiful! Whipped by the wind's fury!'

'There's certainly a wind,' said Mrs Turner dangerously. 'You'll excuse me.' She handed the milk from the ice chest to Miss Symes, and went back to the stove, her basting.

'A couple of *plain* scones.' It was a statement.

Mrs Turner suppressed a sigh and reached for the tin.

'Now John, he's a youngster who's always had plenty of meat, isn't he?' Miss Symes went on, determinedly woman to woman.

'As much as he'd eat, Miss.'

Mrs Turner went on putting the scones onto a plate. Then with a fixed smile she held open the door. Charlotte Symes had to pick up the tray and climb the steps that led to the rest of the house.

After two hours both pupil and teacher were tired. Little progress had been made and, thinking it over, she decided to resort to something that flew in the face of all her many and long-considered beliefs about education.

'Jessie.' She played an arpeggio with passion and waited until the notes had died away. 'Don't you think this will be of use to you. Stephen's learning too, you know. Now think.' There was silence. Jessie stared all around the large room and finally at Miss Symes' warm face.

'Just imagine, next time he visits you'll be able to play to each other. Or play duets. Playing duets together . . . you'll love it. I used to play with my sister when we were young. Oh it's such fun!'

'What's a duet?'

Nonetheless it seemed to have the effect Charlotte Symes had intended.

Monday morning before school. Jessie and John Turner stood together on the steps outside the kitchen, waiting for Mrs Turner to finish their school lunches.

'How many people do you reckon would have warts?'

'In the whole world?'

'No, in the whole country.'

'Well, I've got them an' so's dad.' John paused, his square face screwed up with concentration.

'Two.'

'And mum, only hers went away.'

'Three. They'll come back you know.' Jessie thought of those hands cutting her sandwiches.

'Mum reckons they won't. She rubbed them with string and buried the string.'

'Where'd she bury it?'

John looked at the ground.

'Can't tell or it won't work.'

Jessie stood up on the top of the kitchen steps and began to jump down backwards. A step, a question.

'OK, who else?'

'Johnny Wise, Fred Carpenter. His is huge – we call it his extra finger. He really has a paddy.'

'If you touch a wart you get a wart. Girl's are never so bad. Only Laura Reilly has them in our class.'

'Most of the boys have them. I reckon hundreds of kids must have them.'

'If you get a wart on y'tongue you die.'

'Who says?'

Jessie had reached the bottom step.

'Race you to the gate and I'll tell you who says.'

There was another child in that garden's acres and she had found him.

After school there was cake and milk in the kitchen with John. It would be fruitcake or jam roll or sometimes scones with jam if Mrs Turner was in a good mood. John would tell his mother about his homework, unpacking his bag as he talked. He was always talking about his homework. Food was something very important for John too; he always told his mother what he had liked and what he had not liked in his lunch. Although he never left any she noticed.

Jessie went alone to the front of the house and greeted Miss Symes whose face brightened. She interrupted her book to take Jessie's hands. She brushed Jessie's pinafore and pulled her hair ribbon straight. She looked at Jessie's face for a moment. She was always so glad to see you. And you were a little bit glad, but only that, to see her.

'Begin with your scales dear. I shall come over in a minute.'

A cake crumb found on your tooth and sucked throughout the lesson was the only reason you kept going. Every bit of clumsiness could be heard out loud. She longed for her hands to dance on the keys the way she felt Miss Symes' hands did. She didn't want the slow stumbling from bar to bar that being all her hands could manage, lost the melody before it was finished, the long silences between one note and the next. Sometimes over the first few months she would hear a phrase coming from her own hands that would delight but more often she merely plodded horribly on.

Afterwards, Charlotte Symes felt triumph, yes, triumph over how she had managed to be patient. Despite Jessie's difficulties she *was* improving. There was a strange pleasure, almost a thrill, in having to be patient, in all its forms. She might rejoice when Jessie mastered a difficult passage without a mistake or began to play some of the more difficult scales; she also rejoiced every time she stifled a sigh or patiently played through the part for the left hand an octave too high as they sat together on the piano seat.

It was an old piano with a beautiful tone Miss Symes said. Once as Jessie played she was overcome by the urge to abandon the little piece set before her (with the numbers above the composer's name marking the date on which she had begun to learn the study) and take off on a theme that would take in everything, that would allow her hands to dart all over the keyboard, that would say everything the little pieces could never say in the spaces of that room with Miss Symes watching.

When she did this, angry discords sounded, rough among

the books and furniture of the room. There was no beautiful theme, no harmony, only flight.

'Jessie, Jessie, such temper!'

Miss Symes sent her to her room to 'recover herself'.

The door shut behind her, Jessie lay on her bed glad to put her shoes on the quilt (which she knew was forbidden), her face pushed into the pillow. Eventually she went to the window and saw below, in the late afternoon light, the distant figure of John hunting for snails, for which he was paid a penny a hundred, among the agapanthus along the drive.

Jessie and John passed through the gates and were about to set off to school. John stopped.

'Can I trust you not to dob?'

'Of course.' What could she dob about?

'Then I'll show you the track to school. It's much more fun. You see the pigs. They charge you.'

He stepped off the road into the bush. Looking at his bag on his back, Jessie followed. It didn't sound very nice, being charged by pigs. But John had not been hurt and anyway she was as brave as John.

Cracking scrolls of fallen bark and sliding on tussocks they went down the slope. Jessie felt they must be lost. Trees rose straight up all around them on their grey trunks, sunlight lent where it could, striped by white bark, shattered by canopies of gum leaves. Then all of a sudden they were on another, rougher, road.

There was a terrible smell, a lavatory smell.

'Just along here.' John smiled happily.

There was a clearing and a little house made of timber.

'Finnegans,' John waved a hand.

Mary, in our class, Jessie thought. And then she saw the barren paddocks of mud past the house and understood the smell. It surrounded them now, as thick as the smells of cabbage cooked in winter in the kitchen with all the windows shut.

As they walked closer and closer Jessie heard the beginning of a chorus of sound, a sound like a breath taken in too quickly, a shrill gasping, the sound you might imagine a baby to make if you pinched his fat. A pool of babies would have to be whipped to produce all that terrible sound.

'As soon as they seen us,' said John exultantly. 'Mr Finnegan feeds them here about now,' he volunteered. 'They think it's him.'

The gasping voices lumbered down the paddock and boiled and bumped against the fence. They don't even care about each other Jessie thought, seeing two smaller pigs hoisting themselves to their feet out of the patina of earth and shit. The torrent of pigs shivered into a foam of pink bodies, balked by the fence but complaining, demanding, something, anything; now. Desperate eyes looked at her as the hills of flesh jostled for a piece of the fence. Jessie stepped back. The eyes were animal eyes. But the flesh was pale, not hide, not hair but pale like her own. Without the fence she would have been knocked down into that shared mess of black mud and worse. A dozen of those holed snouts would have gobbled along her legs long before others chewed their way into her case to her lunch. A larger pig hoisted black trotters onto the bottom railing. Pigs would squash you easily, she thought.

All around them, jerking up into the still blue morning, rose the terrible cries of rage and greed.

'We'd better go or we'll be late,' said John suddenly.

After that they often walked to school by the pig track. They would look at each other outside the gates of the house and set off through the trees without saying a word.

Jessie never told Miss Symes.

'Who made all this, all this garden?' Jessie wondered. It was spring. Miss Symes who was cutting flowers and laying them in a long flat basket, allowed herself a careful smile. The child was thriving and there were years yet for her to outgrow what could be called impetuosity.

'It is a beautiful garden isn't it. A fitting embellishment for the house. My father planned it, Jessie. His name was Octavius, Octavius Symes.' She paused.

'He must have been strong,' Jessie said.

'Oh, he didn't do it by himself. He had men to help him. Of course nowadays you couldn't have whole teams of gardeners like he did. They'd want to be paid far too much these days!' Jessie looked at the distant figure of John's father bent over an unweeded bed.

'I'm afraid I've really just followed on, keeping the beds weeded, the fountain clean, the right trees clipped and the delicate ones watered. Father was an amateur naturalist of some distinction. He also explored several remote regions of South Australia in his youth, you know, Jessie. Had some close shaves with the blacks, I believe. But his real distinction, his real love was always botany. He became the best-known botanist in the state.'

'In the world?'

'Oh, I don't know about the world,' Miss Symes laughed, dismissing the world. 'He saw to it that Letitia and I were well educated, in scientific matters,' she added gravely.

It sounded like being firmly corseted, not pleasant but necessary, Jessie thought. They paused by a red rhododendron. Jessie looked at the flowers which grew already gathered, in magenta posies, the colour of celebration. Where was *her* father? What had become of him? Miss Symes walked on.

'He did not educate Letitia and me from any feeling of disappointment that we were not boys, but because he passionately believed in the education of women. He was also among those who had advocated and lived to see all the colonies unite into a federation. I expect you've heard about that at school. He enjoyed this union. I remember, well . . . sharing the triumph of Federation on his arm; he was one of those behind it all along.'

There was a long silence.

'I was . . . restless for several years after his death. I went overseas, visiting distant relatives in England and America. Men and women who had known father's work and had sympathized with his objectives.'

Miss Symes gave a little laugh. 'I myself have not specialized in any area . . . yet.' Her voice trailed off. 'Poetry and music are my real loves, but science, of course, is so important. One shouldn't narrow one's interests too young.'

You would have to stay like a book, Jessie thought, pages flat, opened apart, spine weakened, not to want to run and shout towards some things and not others.

'Shall I teach you how to press flowers dear?' Miss Symes was saying with her child's smile.

'Yes, father really was a very distinguished man.'

6

Miss Symes brought her the telegram and put her hand on Jessie's shoulder.

'I'm sorry, very sorry dear. It seems to be a time of loss for so many people. Apparently he did ask for you both. If that's any comfort.'

She went out, closing the door. Jessie had been colouring a map of Great Britain. She had reached Wales, and was taking special care not to let the pink colour run across the border. She read the telegram and then sat at the desk, trying to think what it all meant. Holding the telegram in her hand she seemed to see it all.

It was several hundred miles north, an isolated sanatorium for those with infectious diseases. Father lay on the sunny verandah in a cane chaise-lounge surrounded by the spare comforts of a public ward. The verandah had remarkable views of the desolate mountains, the ranges that rose out of the plain, pleating the fabric of an ancient cloth. Occasionally, one of the nurses would have time to stop and rest, and, leaning against the verandah, would remark, to the patient nearest her, how beautiful the colours of the sunset were on the mountains.

Father had few such moments. His days and nights were usually passed in fits of coughing and spitting she supposed, interspersed with feverish sleep full of dreams and nightmares. Once, months ago, he had called for his children. They had not come.

There had been more silence than conversation all along. He was an ill-tempered patient, an uncouth man, and the nurses managed, somehow, to convey this to the visiting priest who sat with his hat in his hand beside the iron bedstead.

The room had vases of flowers placed here and there on the white-painted furniture but it was unclear who obtained most benefit from these, the patients or the visitors. Most of the patients seldom had visitors. A few left the hospital, cured, and returned to the city, but most died there.

One such was father. Jessie remembered his farewell years ago, his arms and rough chin. The town on the river was like a distant dream as she sat at her homework in this silent house. Had that other life been real or was only this real? How could both be real? Oh, how had he died? Who had found him? Was his face turned to one side, away from the view?

She was not to know that he was buried in a pauper's grave, and his clothing burnt. Only the matron and the priest attended his funeral and his headstone bore no mention of all those years of ordinary work, no record of all the work of his hands, only dates and his name.

There were days when there seemed to be a pattern and then days when there was no pattern. Events would be like leaves in the wind. Concrete clanged, gravel crunched, boards sounded back the very tread of your feet and carpet would not answer at all. You were eleven, almost grown-up, a year older than last year. When it came to forms, other children had parents but you had a guardian. Lots of things were too childish, too young to interest you anymore.

The best thing was thoughts. She remembered when she was younger, perhaps as little time ago as last year, a thought would alight in her head and immediately flap out through the open door of her mouth. She would hear the beginning of the words before she knew what the end of the thought was. In all the disorder which that brought, other people might learn what you meant before you knew yourself. Only when no one was there were you assured of safety. But now thoughts could sit quite easily behind your eyes.

Watching the teacher in the classroom, the outside person would do what the teacher asked without any questions. But you could think about the teacher, could think anything you liked about the moles on her neck (they were round and black, like spots of mould) or her glasses (they made her eyes as large as the beady eyes of a fly) simply while looking at her as she bent over your work or wrote on the board.

It was the same now with Miss Symes. You saw her in the room as you came in and it didn't matter who was there. Sometimes it was the school teacher, or the minister or even the old, old man, Mr James who was Stephen's guardian. But you could walk into the room and sit or talk knowing exactly who they were, and that your thoughts would stay hidden inside, to be taken out later and spread and smoothed until every thread in the pattern was clear.

Miss Symes never guessed your thoughts. She had a little speech about bringing everything into the open. But if you trundled any old thoughts out she would be satisfied. She liked to talk. But she had 'opinions'. She didn't ever really see what her listener was thinking. Mrs Turner, Jessie thought, anyone could see from her face how much she disliked Miss Symes under the surface. But Miss Symes would never know. She had been trained in scientific fact. She was confident she knew about everything. And because of this she would never know, never guess.

On windy days the sun would come in and out so that the light in the room changed from bright to dark. That was like opening and shutting your eyes. Jessie felt her lashes warm on her cheeks. Then she opened her eyes, zip, and saw the sun lying on top of the clouds again through the top of her window.

She lay in bed, warm from her neck to her toes. It was too early to get up. She felt her feet lying like two warm sleeping dolls down at the foot of the bed. Or almost the foot. She might stretch and still not reach the foot. Her feet wriggled and made those two mountain peaks a long way away but not yet at the bottom of the bed. But much further down the bed than last year.

Today was Saturday, one of Stephen's Saturdays. She brought her hands up to her nose. There was the cut on her right knuckle that had healed into a flat white scar, there was the group of freckles exactly like the southern cross. Or so Dorothy Smith had told her at school. Why did your hands always smell the same, a secret smell that was your own, that told you who you were, never wrong, never failing?

She put her two hands across and around her body until they met in the middle. Through her flannel night-dress both hands felt the secret dimple of her navel. If you pressed hard you got a pain for an instant deep inside as though you were pulling a string. She let her hands lie in peace, one comforting the other so that her elbows lay in the channel of warmth her body made. She was a parcel and her hands were the bow in the centre.

She opened her eyes and looked at the clouds. The sun came and went, came and went and the wind hurried the clouds from one side of the window to the other. They were piled high like the foam you could make in the bath by whipping the soap through the water, piled on top of each other like banks of flowers, like Miss Symes' chrysanthemums that had to have their heavy heads tied to posts. The sun went in and out. And then she noticed that the clouds stayed golden on their tops even as her room darkened. She shut her eyes feeling her hands float up and down as she breathed. If you turned your head sideways you could hear your heart. She held her breath so that her hands rested like flapping birds settling in a tree. But still the pounding in her ears went on. She let her breath in and the pounding raced for a moment and then slowed to a walk. What could stop a heart? Mr Whaite's heart had been stopped by a shell in France and that was why Mrs Whaite had become a widow and why she now lived here. She hugged her hands tighter. Mrs Whaite always answered her letters as she had promised.

She stretched her feet further down one at a time. It was like walking while you were lying down. Would her feet reach to the bottom of the bed by next Christmas? She felt like a perfect parcel just as she was, shoulders, tummy and the two walking legs. Eyes shut and hands the bow on the ribbon.

Suddenly her left foot touched the heavy coldness of last night's hot-water bottle. It was horrid, like something dead and forgotten.

And she sprang out of bed and ran across to the window where the sun had warmed everything.

Today was Friday. Today she had to prove no one in the school was as brave on the school bars as she was.

They stood at the end of the playground by the fence, two bars and a horizontal ladder. Beyond the fence the bush crowded close, fertile and fresh, forbidden to the children who ran like hens in a closely pecked bare yard. Certain boys had been known to climb the fence and disappear into the bush. It was an offence punishable by caning and this, and the whispered excitement of what they did together when safely hidden by the trees made the young eucalypts seem a wood, a mystery.

Perhaps because of this, the bars were not always part of the girls' playground. They were on the border, not safe, not supervised, not a female sanctuary from the tepid centre of which you could see in the distance the cruel and noisy kingdom of the boys. They were a place where boys might appear in dangerous knots of two or three to transact some secret business with girls. Mary Finnegan and Clancy Smith had met there and broken off in front of a small group of supporters from either side.

All week the excitement and tension of the competition had mounted. Now it whirled around the girls like the colours of a Catherine wheel, ephemeral yet blinding.

A line of girls stood near the bars. One or two younger girls even hung by their arms, running to and from the bars to the shouts of the crowd. Jessie tried to look as brave as she felt. She looked at May Edwards, her rival, and May looked back, full of spite, grinning.

For a moment it seemed ridiculous. Do I look as mean as May, Jessie wondered?

But even as she thought this she was walking towards the left-hand end of the overhead bars. It was the better end she had always thought. The grey metal was slippery, there were no thorns of metal, no scars on the left end. To your hands in the sun of midday, the bar felt warm and smooth. In a moment they were both up, poised on top of the bar, one leg over and one leg under. Jessie wrapped her tunic around under her leg. Already a group of boys led by John Turner had gathered at a little distance to watch.

For a moment they sat, one leg crooked, one leg hanging straight down towards the ground like two birds on the same branch, high above the crowd who watched in the summer silence.

To win you had to endure the bar jumping against you with the other girl's swing. You had to go on and on past counting.

Before the word had had time to become a thought, Dorothy Smith had shouted, 'Go'. They were off. Jessie began to fall and whirr, round and round, eyes shut, hands locked, head low. Somewhere in some centre she knew that she was counting, six, seven, eight.

All she had to do was get to fifteen. No one had ever reached fifteen. It was more than May could do. At fifteen, ten, eleven, twelve she could walk away the winner, the best.

But now she felt the tiny counting light begin to falter, fractured by darkness that closed in around it. Go on, go on, the little light sputtered, just a bit longer. No, she would have to stop. Don't think about falling off, keep the swing, go on.

And then she felt the bar jolt and knew that May had swung down and that she was freed, she could swing down clutching the bars to stop herself falling while her friends crowded round to hold her, shouting to her darkened head that she had won, she was the winner in front of the whole school.

When she walked home that afternoon all the triumph she felt had vanished. It was nothing, a school kid's trick, that was all.

He wouldn't be coming to visit every second Saturday any more. He was fourteen. Mr James had said he showed no promise and had sent him away to work in the mid-north. Miss Symes said it would be the making of him. Jessie had to turn away. Why did he need making? He was Stephen, all she had.

She wrote to him now. Miss Symes gave her stationery and stamps. Jessie told him all about school, about the teacher and the other girls. She wrote every week on Sunday night when you could see the week for what it had been.

After several months a letter came from Stephen. Jessie, light with happiness, ran up the gravel drive to the verandah where Miss Symes was watering. She smiled briefly and gave it back to Jessie who read the smudged and pencilled message on the back of the post-card.

Dear Jessie,
How are you old thing? I am well. I like working for Mr Fenson. We have almost finished getting our harvest in. We had a very hot spell recently, some people round here are already carting water. How is your schoolwork going? When do you finish with school? I'm off to the war as soon as I am of age.

Your brother,
Stephen

It was like being winded, a blow where a blow should never be. Jessie was filled with a slow sinking feeling. She put the post-card in the pocket of her old cotton pinafore, groped her way to a chair and stared out across the valley. It was early morning on a hot summer's day. From the verandah, you could see out across the careful lawns, the fountain, the walls and palms and the drive to the orchard and beyond that, through the branches of gums, to the ranges and the city on the plains below. Stephen was all she had. He was too young to go to war. If he went to the war he would be killed. Sooner or later everyone would be killed in the war. In the paper the lists covered column after column. It took Miss Symes half an hour to read all the names as she dutifully chewed her breakfast. She always knew someone. One day the name she knew would be Stephen's. She saw the back of his head all of a sudden with terrible clarity, the way his fair hair grew from the crown, beneath it the flesh and bone she loved so dearly. Father was dead, mother would never come back; he was all she had. She saw his face, so calm and kind, suddenly turned by a horror of approaching death, some bullet or shell that he couldn't dodge. One second of knowledge, one second of clarity and then death. The change in his face for that second would last in her mind for the rest of her life; that look, for him a moment, his last moment of time, for her a nightmare that would never end.

'Impossible to sit on the verandah,' Miss Symes said gaily, 'and not be transported out of oneself, to feel the influence of higher things.'

There was a silence. Miss Symes gave a sidelong glance at the child and the untouched grubby sewing on the table.

'Don't get emotional, Jessie. He'll not be old enough for years,' she said. Jessie, startled, looked at Miss Symes and smiled. That lady felt more than annoyed that the subject should bring such pleasure and, rather irritated, told Jessie not to dream but to persevere with her sewing. Before Jessie bent her head over the wandering stitches again she saw, as she could not have seen a minute ago, how blue the sky gleamed beyond the trees.

Why didn't he write longer letters? Why didn't he write more often?

She had fallen asleep last night weighed down by those thoughts, dreaming about them as if they were crows that called and cawed, circling forever without any landing, any perch.

Now she lay, neither asleep nor awake hearing the dawn begin, certain in the dark of her familiar bedroom that she heard something wonderful, seeing all the harsh questions of the night before settle and shuffle, not oily black like the fabric of crows but ivory weight, the angel's wing, heaven's cloak.

Outside the window it was still dark but the shape of the curtain showed the half light of dawn. She never woke at this hour. She liked to sleep on until the sun had crept across the floor and then close her eyes until they opened without thought or effort on their own. But now she couldn't go back to sleep, now she would never drift off because the music had begun, more beautiful than anything she had ever heard, without explanation or cause.

It seemed to start far away as if it came in a great curve around the horizon of the earth, as if all the world you knew when you stood on the highest hill could be bowed or plucked to set forth some perfect harmony. The horizon curved without flaw, as though you were a stone and your farthest sight a ripple's perfection from the centre of your eyes' glance. And this sound came and came again, wave after rising wave, so distant at first that she thought it part of a dream, something she had merely imagined and would not want to lose. But her eyes were open. Now she heard the sound rising in the long repeated perfect curve, a choir that sang and sang to her alone. Her room was utterly still. The curtains slept with the house, turned to stone.

And then she knew. There could be no other cause. She saw them rise, far-off and magnificent, moving with the night as if they lifted it around the basin of the world, a darkness retreating before the sun's every step. Long-winged and sandalled, brown-winged and gold, the stern-faced singing of angels. She would never hear it again. She had never heard it before. Somewhere, far away, he rose in the dawn on that farm she would never see, well and happy. Letters were only letters. He would write. He would not die. That was why she heard now the voice of the angels again and again ringing against the curved edge, tongue to the bell, perfection, striking on celestial chords that old metal, earth, as she lay awake, scarcely breathing, afraid of her joy.

Never again would she know that harmony. She would try to awaken in time but never did. It was always too early, the night's silence, or too late: the familiar land calls of roosters to wing-clipped hens in muddy sheds.

On a Saturday afternoon in autumn all tiny Stirling knew that Maisie Smith had married a soldier.

Jessie stood in the crowd at the church gates, waiting for

the bride and groom to appear. Would Miss Symes have let her gawp? She thought not. But Miss Symes believed she was out searching for wild orchids in the bush below the house. She would never know.

Half the girls in the school were there. But only you had a best friend who was a bridesmaid. In the drab little group of children in their Saturday pinafores that gave you a huge sense of importance. Why, you were almost part of the wedding party. Dorothy had been your best friend for a year. She had promised to tell all about it.

Jessie had seen the pale bride hurry in to the church's gloom. Outside, as all the women agreed, it was the loveliest of autumns. Yes, quite the best autumn colours they could remember. Sun warmed the backs of the children strung along the fence and tried in level beams to catch the yellow and red confetti of leaves that drifted down, spiralling with infinite grace on unseen currents. Half bare, the great oaks and beeches stood, waiting, waiting. A leaf landed with a sound as soft as a kiss.

Music suddenly boomed from inside the church and then the bride and groom appeared, arm in arm, smiling, the bride's veil no longer hiding her face like the net that kept flies out of the sugar but thrown back over her shoulders. The crowd murmured. The couple stopped on the steps. A man Jessie had never seen before began taking photographs. The bride and groom smiled and smiled.

Jessie had forgotten Dorothy. She stared at the bride and groom. They were married. They stood smiling together. And yet they looked so different. The man was red-faced with hair so short it was almost as though he had a shaven head. His ears were red, the colour of autumn leaves. He wore a khaki uniform, belted and buttoned. And how he filled it! Jessie thought his buttons might burst off, like a shower of coins on the road. He wasn't a fat man but he filled the dense wool stuff of the uniform as if he were as hard as a tree and the uniform his tight bark. He had shiny shoes, man's shoes. That was the groom.

The bride was a meringue of falling lace and tulle. Layers of veil fell away over her shoulders, lacy froth trimmed her neck, wrists and hem. She might not have bones or legs at all, Jessie thought. Perhaps that was why she clung to the woollen arm and leant in towards him. In one hand she held a huge bunch of flowers and they too were white and soft, the trailing gypsophila and sprays of tight ruffled rosebuds almost hidden in the folds of lace on her dress. Around her neck she wore flat milky-white pearls, docile gems without the power to reflect or sparkle.

And yet these two who could not be more apart were married and now walked off together in a shower of rice, pale autumn for them alone.

He was different. He wasn't the old Stephen. Or perhaps it was her, perhaps I'm different.

To decide before falling asleep suddenly seemed very important. He was here, in Miss Symes' house somewhere, asleep, staying for two precious days that should have been jewel-bright. And yet they had not been at all.

How cool he was and tall in long trousers, so that she felt awkward, a girl running about with plaits down her back. She was going to tell him so many things but none of them now seemed important.

They walked all afternoon far from the house on the crest of the ranges, below them a spill of smaller hills, then the city on its plain, distant and impossibly vast. And beyond the city –

'There,' she cried. 'I'm sure – yes you can see it – just. That glint. It's the sea!'

But he had only glanced and then looked down at her. 'Possibly.'

And she had had to run to catch up with him.

'You're not very ladylike – yet.'

'Ladylike?'

'Isn't that what you're supposed to be. And be grateful you've been taught so.'

She hadn't thought of that.

'Symes.' He laughed and gestured back at the house. 'One of the "old families". They never let me forget it; that he married a Symes.' That they are 'connected' to the Symes.

'Not like us. Irish.' He paused and said in a voice that Jessie suddenly recognized as Mr James': '"Of course, Catholics, Irish, what can you expect." Does she say things like that to you?'

'No. She only talks about what her father was. Never about me.'

'Lucky you!'

'She likes me, Stephen.'

He was silent.

'Who cares whether they like us or not!'

The wind caught them on the crest, washing their clothes against their bodies or ballooning them out so that their legs stuck out like sticks. Stephen shoved his cap in his pocket and Jessie's hat, tied around her neck, pulled and flapped. She dragged a stick along the track enjoying the lines it made and wanted to race along the winding stretch of track. If she thought about it, it was like a low light, Miss Symes' affection, unnoticed but enough. He had been silent, his face bitter when she looked up at him. Who had changed, and when had the change happened?

It was hours later, and she must have slept. A pain drilled in her head near her ear and with the clarity of someone half-asleep she went to Stephen's room through the darkness of the house. There he lay, thin and childish, the brother she had always loved, lost to all bitterness, one arm cradling his head.

He awoke slowly and grumpily filled his own hot water bottle, wrapped it in his jersey and gave it to Jessie to put near her ear. She slept for a while and then awoke consumed by the ache, trying not to cry.

And then he came again, appearing in the darkness of her room wrapped in a blanket. He stroked her hair and sat beside her bed in an old chair, his chin at his knees, his poker face above the blanket's bulk. The pain dulled, Jessie slept and then awoke, how much later, she could not imagine since she had thought she had been awake, silent, watching his face. But she awoke to find his face, wordless, calm and benevolent, watching her own as she opened her eyes to the dark; on his face, shadowed by the darkness, nothing changed, nothing that she had not known and loved as long as she remembered knowing anything at all.

Sewing in the evenings for the Fighting Forces Comforts Fund it seemed, now that you were twelve, anything might be discussed. So tonight they were talking about marriage. Miss Symes needed very little prompting.

'There was a . . . suitor . . . indeed. A young man – or so I thought –   It was five years after father's death. I met him at a ball. He tried to persuade me to dance which I would not do of course. I talked to him at fêtes and public lectures at the Town Hall. He seemed then to be always hovering nearby at the functions I went to. I . . . came to like him considerably.' Miss Symes looked down at the heel she was turning and frowned. 'All along, though, I felt he should have more gravity and solemnity, I mean a man my own age.' She frowned again. It sounded like buying something, Jessie thought. Miss Symes ploughed on. 'But I was ready to accede to his wish to know me better, and his position and family made this in every sense a suitable wish I should add. But then I received a shock.' There was a long silence. Of course, Jessie thought, he was already married.

'Oh, it was just a casual remark. Overheard through the leaves of a potted palm at a soirée. I found out that he was ten years my senior.' She paused. 'This made me determined to avoid him in future. Ten years, what had he done with those ten years! He should have been able to guide and direct me. But I felt he was weak, weak underneath. So that was that.'

She put down the sock and began to rummage in the pile for her larger needles. Jessie looked at her from above a long line of stitches. There would not be any more suitors. But what about his smile she wondered, amazed. What about his hair and hands? I don't know what he looked like, I only know how he was to be rejected. Perhaps that was what you learnt. All the things that were wrong, all the things that were not right, so that when a man appeared you could decide what was wrong about him while he was at a safe distance. There seemed to be a lot of tests a man had to pass. And you spent years learning the tests so that you could judge him.

When she reached the end of the row, another thought appeared, wrecking this smooth understanding like a dropped stitch discovered too late to be picked up. What if the man passed all the tests, what did you do then?

Standing in front of the stove Jessie felt a tight shell of fear and confusion. Cooking was hard. She was supposed to be making a white sauce in a small saucepan next to Mrs Turner's large one. But already her butter had gone a horrid dark brown and now her flour lay in sullen lumps in the milk.

'Turn down the heat.'

Jessie reached for the tap and turned it the wrong way so that gas leapt out, viciously blue, around the base of her saucepan. She would never get it right. The saucepan handle, heated by the flame, burnt her hand. Tears began to make a lump in her throat. Mrs Turner, adding nutmeg, had, at least, noticed nothing. She never did.

You were supposed to be learning to cook because Miss Symes liked to think that it was an accomplishment. To Mrs Turner's face she had briskly said, 'An accomplishment equally as important as the piano.' Somewhere Jessie knew that it was really a hedge against the growing embarrassment she felt at admitting to her acquaintance that she was teaching Jessie the piano.

Jessie finished the white sauce, squashing the lumps with a fork and stirring until it was smooth. Mrs Turner scraped it into the big saucepan and then set Jessie to washing up. Thank goodness, an easy task, one that she liked. She spent long half hours at it, keeping the basin in the sink brimming with water, whipping the yellow pieces of soap inside their metal cage till the water frothed, washing the sink. She came to know all the little marks in the enamel draining board much as she knew the moles on her own short arms. And you could think as you did it.

Will I ever make a white sauce well? Months had passed since she had begun to be taught. All her life she felt she would never be the sort of person who learnt which way the taps turned, up or down. But why did you need to be that sort of bustling person? You could easily adjust taps, by watching the steam twisting from the saucepans, observing its dying or ferment and seeing in its clouds, your thoughts.

'Now Dorothy's dead the house will be sold. Mr James says it's too large. I don't want to live there now. And besides if a fellow doesn't go soon the whole show will be over.'

So he would go to the war, and he told her now as they were walking in the garden, Jessie in her best longer skirt made and worn to celebrate his visit. She sat on the edge of the pond, her face shadowed by the fountain that never played. She couldn't trust herself to speak.

'I saw Mrs Whaite at the funeral. Ordinary woman isn't she.

Though I'm sure she's very nice,' he added hastily.

'She re-married,' Jessie said from some arctic necessity.

Sun streaked the lawns, the water in the pond mirrored the pale June sky. The house towered behind them, a stone edifice of shadows and on the verandah Miss Symes sat by her teapot, watching her garden with Olympian eyes that saw no human tears. They hardly cast a shadow walking on the lawns, and neither did they feel the cold or the sun. And yet they were mortal. He was her flesh and blood.

'I'm sorry you're going. It's foolish.'

'Did she ask after me?' Jessie added, thinking of Mrs Whaite in Goodwood, that suburb most typical of any in the city on the plain.

'Oh yes. I told her you were quite the young lady, these days.'

I suppose I am, she thought, but still felt the tears, the pain. They had stopped near the rhododendron hedge, blooming as Octavius Symes had planned it. Every green limb brandished a white gloved fist, next month's blossoms; leaves as heavy as angel's feathers in an old icon drooped obediently towards the ground. He was flesh and blood and could not be protected. Looking at the rhododendron leaves she remembered the story of the twelve brothers turned into swans, the sister and the jackets of nettles, the brother left with one sleeve unfinished, one arm a swan's wing forever. And yet he was smiling, could tell her lightly.

'Don't worry about me – over there – will you?'

She wanted to shake off the arm he casually put around her shoulders and shout at him not to go.

'Miss Symes won't like you to know this. I ran away from that farm.' Stephen looked up at the verandah. By common agreement they walked away from the stately drive towards the back gardens.

They sat on the wall together, their feet dangling above the rhubarb.

'This is more you and me.' He was smiling so that her heart

tipped towards some vortex.

'What was it like? You never wrote, I mean you never really said.'

She had never complained before, so much did she long for the three or four cards a year from this brother. He jumped down and stood behind the wall with his elbows on the top. Long shadows from the saplings in the paddock fell across all the rows of cabbages and potatoes. He looked up into her face as she sat.

'What's the point of letters? You can't change things by writing about them. I couldn't describe what it was like. I couldn't see the point of letters.'

She searched his face. Should she care so much. Did he? But he would be leaving soon. She might not see him for a long time. She pushed away his response and the answers that it had begun to provoke in the back of her mind; she would think about it later.

It was late. They walked back to the house and Miss Symes admonished Stephen who was hard-pressed to catch the train.

'Theodore will wonder where you are.'

Stephen half ran down the steps to Mr Turner and the trap but at the gate he turned and waved wildly to Jessie, even at that distance looking her straight in the eye.

'It's time for music practice Jessie. And don't fold your arms like that. It's not done.'

'We don't want to lose you. But we think you ought to go.'

They stood on the noisy asphalt of the wharf and Jessie did not know what to say. The troop ship in the background was a giant sideshow of action as men in uniform clustered along the sides and clambered about the bulkheads. Stephen, tall, tanned and manly in his uniform looked, to Jessie, very grand, completely grown-up.

She, too, was in a new longer dress as befitted a girl of

thirteen; she had been sewing it for weeks, with Miss Symes' help. Stephen had even told her how pretty she looked. They were surrounded by crowds of uniformed men.

The women were in white and pastels, their best dresses and parasols. The men wanted to be off: for the women every moment longer on the wharf was one more grain of time before the inevitable.

Stephen was young. He had put his age up with Mr James' consent and now stood tall and slender in khaki, holding his sister's hand and glancing at the other men. Jessie tried to commit to memory every aspect of his open face beneath the strange profile of the hat. When he had to leave, he shook Miss Symes' hand and in a touch that startled her, saddened her and finally made her feel old, thanked her for looking after his sister.

'I'll write. Wish me luck Jess.' One hug and he walked towards the gangway. Jessie could hardly believe he was irrevocably gone.

Even Miss Symes on occasion might respond to the mood of the public and so they stayed on the wharf while the band played and Stephen waved to Jessie. She turned her face to the sea and watched until the boat's course made the individual men on the ship just a mass of indistinguishable bodies.

With a little lecture about plants and then different sorts of animals Miss Symes had explained it before it happened. The talk was not without its awkward moments but Miss Symes had kept it very scientific as she had intended. No need for any silliness. But how, Jessie thought, going out of the back door with her disguised bundle, how did those words relate to this, all this?

She walked across to the laundry, a little stone building which had once been the kitchen, and hoping that Mrs Turner or John would not appear. She turned on the taps. Wisps of blood trailed through the water like smoke. Red flowers wavered in the current and reached towards the surface, pink blossoms spread from wall to concrete wall of the tub. And you had to put your hands into that, amongst those rags, black-shaped, bent with blood.

She remembered looking around the class at the girls only last week. Dorothy had already 'started'. And at Dorothy's house, quite by accident she had seen a bundle of rags, waiting to be washed in the laundry.

One moment she had been playing hide and seek. The next moment she had stopped, heart thudding. Who had been injured? It was the bandages from a terrible wound. In the dust of the laundry she looked at the familiar cake of yellow soap, the dented lid of the copper. But then that? In the stillness she stared and stared and thought the shock would never wear away.

She ran out and hid behind the apple tree. But next day at school she looked at all the girls and thought, who? Which ones? They all ran and skipped. But some must have that secret. All women did.

It meant you were grown-up, she thought. You left something and joined something else.

Violets in flat trays of water carried their thin scent out of the room, back to the garden. Huge bunches of jonquils stood up to their green and white necks in buckets of water. Daffodils, really far too many, but people had to bring something, Miss Symes thought, stood in their tins in patient lines down the garden path. Inside, the rarer irises were being pinched out to be the blue of red, white and blue posies. Over everything rolled the perfume of daphne and hyacinths, flowers that looked as though they were made of wax, needing to fell the senses with their heavy scent.

The women and girls flowed in and out, all wearing aprons.

It was like a festival Jessie thought, all this talk and laughter, and activity. John appeared, every so often with bunches of precious azaleas, embarrassed and anxious to clear off again. Did all these women know how to arrange flowers she wondered, her hands for a moment idle? She had heard nothing from France. But his being so far away, over there, was the reason why she and the other women were here, talking and busy among the flowers.

'Do handle those jonquils with more care John.'

'Here Turner, thank you.'

The district was having a fund-raising fête to help the Fighting Forces Comforts Fund. Jessie's class was to supply posies and Miss Symes, on a clear spring morning, was in command.

'Really, John, haven't you any idea at all how to go about it.'

'Don't bruise the daffodils. Jessie, look, this is how you add the fern – at the back. And I just put a *few* sprigs of blossom on *one* side, not both: it's far too symmetrical.'

Jessie had made dozens of posies already and to her eyes they had all looked perfectly adequate. He might be lying dead in the mud, she thought. They sold bunches of flowers and he might be dead. You could think about the idea of that, let it knock, but not let in the real horror.

'Not so much colour. One or two at the most. Anything else is showy, Jessie.'

Long ago when she was still a child she had believed the angels when she chanced to hear them. And now she knew she had been right.

Not allowed to go with the Turners to the city and not wishing any longer to sit with Miss Symes and the heavy ticking clocks in the emptiness of the curtained drawing-room, Jessie offered to make a cup of tea, and wandered down through the dimly lit hall to the back of the house. Doing the simplest things filled her with a heavy pleasure. Nothing jarred or spilt; lids fitted, water flowed, tea settled in a dark constellation telling a thousand unknown good fortunes. She filled the kettle and put some more wood in the top of the stove with a practised hand, for more and more time was given these days to learning the art of cooking. Piano lessons had somehow long since lapsed.

She went out into the soft November night, and stood by the hydrangeas. Through the cool dark she could hear still the wild ringing of bells from the churches in the village. The war was over, and somewhere in France Stephen lay, recovering in hospital. This much she knew and going back into the warmth of the kitchen, she began to get Miss Symes' supper. It was enough: the world had never been so much hers.

She met him in the heart of the city months later.

'You didn't tell me.'

He tried to stop her crying, buried her head against his chest. No one was staring, he noticed. Perhaps the city had seen it many times: a woman crying on a returned man's uniform.

'Come on now, Jess. Tell me about you. Theodore died; I heard that.'

But her mouth was full of tears and wobbled again.

'A few more days in camp and I'm going to shoot through. Look for work in the West. There's no reason to stay here.'

He looked like someone else. So much older, his face pouched and bagged under his eyes. She could say none of the things she had planned in the train. She would have to learn, smile as he was smiling now, despite those lines.

'What will you do?'

But that's not what I mean, she thought, as she heard the words. They would work. She knew it suddenly and so strongly that she didn't need to mention it. It was why they stood here, having to say goodbye in a crisp March morning, the sky above them high and blue without limit, the world of the teeming square with its expansive vista of paths and trees and unexpected life, only a view, merely scenery.

As Stephen hesitated on the steps, about to go, Jessie saw their parting, suddenly, for all its immediacy, as a sham. They would work. So that even though Stephen was already picking up his bag as her hand reached out to him, she saw they were like characters in a school play who stride off opposite sides of the stage only to meet behind the backdrop. There was no possibility of their futures being unexpected.

'I'm glad you're back.' She was close to tears again and could not manage more than that. He had left everything unsaid but as he walked away, he shouted back across the street, 'I'll write to you, Jess.'

She stood a moment watching him go out into the square in the heart of the city, into the world of men and affairs, his left sleeve flapping, his crippled arm pinned to his chest.

7

Sent like a slow letter by Miss Symes' recommendation, she was going to work for two sisters who lived, she thought gazing out of the smeared window of the bus, at a suitable distance from everything. You descended into the city from the hills and then you climbed out again, keeping the sea to your right. The little bus tugged and clawed at the road, sending dust out onto the grass at the side of the fields. The sea remained now hidden, now glimpsed, while the bus pushed on and on. The land was cleared and the road went south towards the sun, towards stretches of gold.

She sat on the seaward side of the bus. There was something about these vales that seemed familiar. All those years with Miss Symes had been spent amongst forested slopes, gullies and ridges where the wind gossiped from tree to trunk. You had to climb to be able to see any distance. But here time and the wind had scoured the hills and never left them. Anyone could see for miles. The land was exposed magnificent, unafraid, the coat of an old lion, the hills, soft paws resting on the plain.

They had left the city far behind and now journeyed through the afternoon further and further into the sun-coloured fields. Here and there, trees and old stone houses darkened a cleft gully with their greens and greys. Olive trees might dot a hill or pine trees cluster above unmoving sheep, but the rest of the land lay asleep, uncomplicated.

That was it. The world lay open like the half-remembered landscapes behind the town on the river. Now, still looking through the dusty amber of the window, she remembered nothing of that landscape in its details; where trees were found or the directions to a certain house.

But she remembered the feeling. It was land where you would not lose your way. All around you it lay in its great brown and saffron spaces, with the wonderful shadows collecting the colour and changing it to ochre and red. The hills pawed and claimed the plains. Every fold was generous. Warmed by the sun, the hills gave back yellow as gold. You could see for miles. You could see the wind's path before it reached you. You would learn to love the wide curves of shadow and light on the hills as if it were something you owned, a photograph that you could take out and examine when you already knew all its irregularities and patterns of sepia and brown.

The road turned now so that it followed the curve of the hills where they turned towards the sea. But still they were there, crumpled, heavy; curves and folds of an ancient fabric.

So that when she stepped down from the bus to greet the sisters who stood like two peg dolls, there was something already in her step, some power in her hand that flowed from within as she stood there, reliant for everything on the pale hands that extended to take her own.

Why she should love the house so much she could never explain. In it she was a servant, a servant in the servant's bedroom conveniently adjacent to the kitchen. It was a little room with one bed and, as she discovered on her first night, a lumpy mattress. But she adjusted to the lumps in the mattress as one would, she supposed, to sleeping with another person, adjusted her sleep around the shapes that were given.

The room had two windows, one looking out through the back verandah, up past a bank of strong-scented geraniums to the hill behind the house. Across the hill someone had planted three almond trees. They were never beautiful she thought. But when she had been there a year she discovered that they had two moments of beauty. One was when the trunks were black with rain, and the other longer debut when they were covered with wonderful white blossom before the winds of August blew away the fragile beauty, leaving only the sensible tiny stumps that would become paper-shell almonds.

The western window was sheltered by a verandah next to a line of tamarisk trees that were green and sweet in spring and a dusty yellow waste, littering gutter and verandah with dead needles all through the autumn. She couldn't see any further than the stout trunks of the tamarisk trees and the low hedge of wormwood that wound in an untidy row of silver fronds all the way up the side of the hill marking the boundary of the block.

It was a small room without views, a room that defined her niche.

And yet she grew to love it within days.

It was the sound of the sea. All those years, like some forgotten face, she had not realized how much it had been missing on the edge of her life's circle. On her first night in the house as she lay awake in the lumpy narrow bed under the window, she knew herself back home, home in some ancient corridor of the heart.

There were parts of the day when she couldn't hear the sea, moments when she was clattering inexpertly on the stove, spells when the Misses talked in the evenings, over their dinner, punctuating her thoughts as she sat chewing in the kitchen, with the delicate chink of their ivory-handled knives and silver forks. But once she was alone in her own room the sound of the waves flowed in all around her, filling the room like the heart-beat of a memory.

She could listen to each wave following the one before, or await the one to come with its unfailing hiss and fall. In her mind she could see the fast one streaming up the sand and the next waiting further out in a patient succession; anticipated, unhurried, unfailing.

There were moments on the wildest nights when there would be no pause between waves, when the sound of the sea would rage like a temper long since lost. But the nights she loved most were the rare ones when there was silence between wave and unrushed wave, when she waited, half asleep, hearing that brief transitory silence as though something beneficent paused between breath and eternal breath.

Every day except Sunday she awoke in time to take the billy off the front garden gate before the sun had caught it, coming out into the coolness of dawn as the sound of the milkman's horse receded through the quiet lanes. On Mondays she set her alarm even earlier since she was supposed to stoke the fire under the copper before Miss Edith arose. The laundry was in a little shed on one side of the back garden; there was a copper, two tubs and a cold-water tap. A cat with black and white blotches would come and purr around her legs as she broke the sticks and stacked them around the newspaper. It was the best part of the day. After a while she could admit she enjoyed the solitude.

Miss Edith, she discovered, was very particular. Everything had to be done her way. You spent a lot of the morning, while rubbing or rinsing or passing clothes through the mangle, waiting for her next remark. Her corrections were always delivered patiently. She thought she was imparting information of lasting value. And I know it all anyway, Jessie thought, soap suds to her elbows. It was better out of the small damp shed, better hanging out the clothes, working your way down the long lines with the weight of the pegs in your apron pocket, whilst the line sagged behind you under the weight of the wet clothes.

Every wash day had its stations; one of these occurred when the props were put under the lines and the rows of sheets and tablecloths began to flap in the air instead of just clearing the lawn. Away from that white wetness Miss Edith and Jessie ate their scrappy lunch in the kitchen. Then they went out and began the small personal washing: underwear, stockings and blouses. These took so long but at least, she thought drearily, it was not heavy work. Hung out of sight on a low line that ran between the house and one of the trees in the tangled undergrowth to the east of the house, the white garments looked like blossoms against the green. 'We hang them there so they won't be glimpsed by anyone,' Miss Edith explained. Privately, Jessie thought it rather unlikely. No one would ever call on the Misses Wilson on Mondays.

Afternoon and the little timber house was inexpressibly quiet. All you could hear when the washing-up was done were the slow creaks among the timbers of the house and the far-off hissing of the sea. Edith Wilson had disappeared to her bedroom. Jessie guessed that she was asleep although she had indicated that she intended to read.

It would be hard not to sleep in this silence, she thought, listening to the faint sound of the unhurried waves. She lay back on the lumpy mattress but could not sleep. Everything in the Wilson house had to be just so. You had to adjust yourself to a life that was not of your own making and the best of times were always the pauses after one task was done. She had been told how to do everything in detail. This and this and now, the minutes had passed, this.

Precisely at 3.30 p.m., Jessie began preparing afternoon tea, opening the cold little door and putting the milk jug on the tray. Then she put the kettle on the stove and while waiting for it to boil, found in the pantry at the end of the kitchen, the tin of biscuits. Miss Edith stirred at the sound of the kettle. It won't be necessary to drop a spoon or slam a cupboard door Jessie thought, carrying the tray out to the open north-facing front verandah.

It's a ritual she suddenly knew, lifting the tea-cosy for the first time. Afternoon tea and then a 'dip'.

Miss Amelia believed that sea-bathing was beneficial for the skin. Her skin was delicate Miss Edith had agreed. So the two ladies 'took a dip' every day except Sundays and exceptionally cold winter days. They would set off as soon as Miss Amelia came in on her bicycle from the school she taught at two miles further inland.

Now they sat over tea and cake, waiting. Jessie looked at the calm surface of her tea, confined by the delicate bone china. She had remembered the right cups, the right plates and doilies. The silver spoons lay in a decorous queue. And it was not Sunday and not an exceptionally cold winter's day. How precise, how ordered she thought. As if the weather could be defined by a pair of white-skinned women braving the breakers in soft black swimsuits.

The bicycle with its upright, ladylike rider with the small hat and elegant skirt came sailing down the road, swerved around the corner and was pulled to a halt by the steepness of the hill. Miss Amelia jumped off with a little sideways gesture and wheeled her bike in under the side verandah.

'Sometimes she comes and joins us for a cup of tea but usually she wants her swim,' Miss Edith said tenderly.

The township had once been a port renowned for its calm waters, for it was sheltered by a gulf, but now it was just a sleepy little hollow, a fold in the coast, its few scattered houses separated from each other by paddocks of golden grass. The beach was very close, and from one window in the sunroom Jessie had discovered a view of the sea. That blue had been a lode-stone amongst the shale of the landscape's ochre and olive.

They set off out of the little front gate after a period in their rooms shuffling and opening drawers, clad in three-quarter length tea-gowns and carrying towels. A plain swimsuit had been found for Jessie. It came from a drawer with a smell of camphor. How long, she thought with a rush of pleasure, since I saw the sea. Salt will replace that smell of mothballs.

The road beyond the house forked and they took the lower track that sloped down to the sea. The moment they stepped onto the track they could see the shimmer of the sea, the blue horizon a door between the walls of pines. They walked down one side of a valley, below to their right through tangled scrub Jessie saw a creek that sulked behind the sandbar and then spilt out in a fan of shallow rivers to the sea.

'Oh isn't it . . .'

They looked at her, puzzled.

'Always swim to the left of the track,' Miss Edith informed her crisply. After trudging through the sand the sisters stopped.

'Here Amelia?'

'Oh I think so.'

Carefully leaving two heaps of neat belongings, they walked down to the wet edge of the sea.

'We have the beach to ourselves,' Miss Edith said loudly.

The two ladies swam out, keeping close to each other, their heads conversing, water lapping their necks. Jessie wished she could swim. She walked slowly into the shallow water looking back at the mile after mile of biscuit-coloured cliff and the curving seam of sea and sand.

The sea was now green and as calm as glass. The waves tunnelled towards the shore as though some power sighed in resignation beneath all that turquoise silk. Jessie watched her feet dribble into the sand as the wave passed. They disappeared like her knees, and now with a cold clasp, her waist. Inch by inch as she went deeper and deeper her body disappeared, only to be returned to her more alive and real from that salt embrace. But her feet still grated on the sand. She could not trust herself to try.

The Misses' voices swam with careful strokes further out. Miss Amelia's red-gold hair covered by a white bathing cap bobbed on the waves like a floating gull. The sun warmed Jessie's arms to honey. How long, how long she thought since I have known this. Sitting in the water up to her shoulders, staring back at the cliffs and the land beyond, she decided that she would learn to swim.

The landscape was made of simple planes, the bulk of cliffs and hills cut off by the vast flatness of the sand and sea. She heard the two ladies' voices as they swam towards her and she came out, cold and smaller onto the sand. Miss Amelia, who had paler skin than Jessie had ever seen, dried herself quickly, put on her old hat and gown and, pushing her bony white feet into her sandals, set off up the sand. Jessie guessed she was worried about her skin. Miss Edith dried herself more slowly, a short distance from Jessie, with a modestly turned neck, covered in freckles.

'We'll get Colin to teach her to swim,' it was agreed between the sisters.

At night, Jessie would lie in bed half awake, half asleep. With her eyes shut, memory could blow along some wasted stretch towards the bright fullness of the present, as wind blown tumbleweeds might suddenly catch against her as she walked on the beach.

Later in the evenings the wind would die away and then she would hear in the distance through the rustling of the tamarisk trees outside, the far-off endless repetition of the waves. Some nights she would fall asleep, inadvertently, hearing the sound of the waves over and over again as if an imaginary reader somewhere, eyeless, were turning back the pages of a never-ending book with patient searching. The silence was the scrutiny and the little waves' rush the always dissatisfied turning back to an earlier page with some murmured 'not here, not here', and then another rustle as the next page was always turned, passingly perused, and brushed aside.

The noises of the sea could so easily become that other sea so long ago. The room she slept in and the warmth of her bed could dissolve away until there was nothing left but some self, not woman, not child, but some finned traveller on the edge of the deep, suspended between dark and light water, floating between the woman of the present and that tiny child by another sea, asleep with her brother, cradled against the wind. The long woman's legs in their cotton night-dress might melt and dwindle into the small spindly legs of that child, the arms she huddled now around herself might become tiny, it did not matter: the body of Stephen that she held in sleep was a small boy's body of all those years ago.

Perhaps the difference between myself and others, she mused, was not so much my being a package that might be handed on and handled, written about, stamped and processed, second-class, but that my life, my memories, are my own. Although different arms (depending on the years) might comfort you, and though there were always arms (somebody's) that was one side of a purchase, the other of which was stamped with the knowledge that next year the arms would be different, and none of the arms would ever know your past, your memories, or be able to even hazard a guess at any of the reasons why occasionally, like anyone, you sometimes awoke, as now from dreams, came up through the surface to that bright hard light, from some too distant, lost, safe past, the sound of the sea still in your ears and wet upon your cheeks.

February. She awoke in the cool of early morning, switching off the alarm on the first ring. Before sunrise you could always smell the creek, the mud dying on the wind, the frog's throat clicking towards dust, fish feeling their world contract to a muddy pond. The ground outside the house was cracked and dry.

Day succeeded hot day and at the end of the heatwave even the centre of the house was hot. Her first job when she awoke was to block out that heat, to fight the sun, to shut up the house. At night the house stood open, every pore letting in the night's relief, the wind from the river or from the hills, the snaking gully wind.

She looked at a post-card from Stephen as she brushed back her hair. He didn't say whether he'd got her letter. She went quietly across the silent dining-room, out through the doors onto the verandah and began to pull down the windows and slide across the heavy green shutters. She worked her way slowly round the front of the house, knowing every squeak of the windows, glad of the piece of soap in her pocket to coax a stubborn sash to silence. The last room of all was Miss Edith's bedroom which had a wire door opening onto the verandah. All the way around the verandah she crept through an atmosphere of sleep, of bedclothes thrown back and quiet breathing, but she was always most conscious of this when she came to the Misses' bedrooms, for though she never peered in, it was impossible not to glimpse the shirt thrown over a chair, the potty under the bed, and all the disorder and intimacy of the iron beds and another person's sleep.

That person lying snoring, mouth agape, pearl of a shaken-out breast between her night-dress buttons, was a teacher, your employer, someone you had to consult over everything. She crept away.

In the summer when Miss Amelia stayed home and cooked,

Jessie worked in the afternoons for the Gerards. They lived a mile inland in a house with verandahs all around, a space like arms extended in greeting.

At dusk she had to water the garden beds around the stone walls of the house and mind the baby, Victor, before his bath. He was never bathed at any one hour. When it suited her, his mother would appear and scoop him up, her mouth laughing at his waving fists.

She began on the east, away from the sun. The ground near the herb garden was so hot that the water hissed. She let the hose run for a few minutes so that scalding water rushed out onto the lawn. When she felt the icy cold welling up from deep below, she began watering in earnest. The earth lapped up the wetness with a dragon's tongue.

She worked her way along the verandahs. Wisteria grew from the ground on a grey twisted trunk, the set face of age that manacled the railing. She could never get the dry bark wet. Around the base were the twisted ribbons of long dead iris. When she came to the front of the house she could see, all of a sudden, the flat expanse of broken brown clod and the neat rows of vines stretching to the creek. The sun was setting behind the gums along the river, the golden light fell around her, hot enough to make vigour impossible.

Working her way across the front of the house, the sun beat down on her old hat. Coolness was a dream, or would have been had it not trickled from the hose.

The baby trailed behind her, brown, only half dressed. Jessie flicked water at him. He gurgled with surprise and began to run, inventing immediately for both of them a game, knowing with certainty that she would play. Grown-ups existed to play his games. She could run like a child. Mrs Gerard would approve. His fat legs wobbled across the thick grass, she brushed water at the little creases behind his knees, as he shouted his way across the baked long-shadowed lawns; delight, delight into the summer's length.

She went between two houses all summer.

Suppose I were one of the Gerards she thought shelling peas. There were eight and they were all handsome. They fell about from one end of the house to the other, all sizes from Victor at eighteen months to Marlene, a solemn ten, conscious of her beauty.

There would be a photograph of the Gerard family taken with a camera, a Christmas present at the end of that year. In it you could see the children sitting cross-legged on the grass, arranged by their laughing parents, trying to still their exuberance long enough to form an image in black and white. All the children had golden hair that curled in a way you could only envy. The girls were wearing their best. What occasion was it, she thought years later? A birthday or Easter Sunday or perhaps the start of the new year. Over a cloth-covered brick Mrs Gerard had lovingly smocked the fronts of the girls' dresses so that light and shadow were stitched together across the crisp fabric. The children's hair even in the black and white coolness caught the sun. It slid and shone, warmth where there could be none; years later, laughter in the silence. The baby sat proudly balanced by the bulk of his nappy, his navel revealed by the shortness of his shirt, his head turned away from the camera, laughing at his mother with the delight of ignorance around his balding head. And all around him were the other children, healthy arms and sandy-haired legs, hair, once flattened by water, now curling again, arms and faces browned by the sun folding the light into the softness of an elbow or cheek. How they looked at the camera, some laughing too much before the shutter clicked, other staring straight at her nervousness with that curiosity that had yet to learn to stop just short of being cruel.

On one end of the row of children sat Mr Gerard and Edith and Amelia Wilson. She couldn't remember how long it had taken her, that photograph. Whatever time, it was long enough for the adults to carefully compose their faces, to smooth down skirts, remove frowns and doubts and put on the face that could be recorded for ever. The children stared, fascinated in their laughing differences by the camera, the moment; those grown-up faces knew not that moment in all its sunniness, only permanence, the record, the image that would endure the years.

At the other end of the row stood the dark-eyed man who worked on the farm, Colin Gerard.

The road stretched back into the hot afternoon. There, gold; there, the sea.

When she heard the counterpoint of the children's voices, Colin's deep among their falsetto, she came to the gate and joined them on their way to the beach.

Their faces bobbed around the tall figure of the man as they walked down to the sea. At every second step one of the children crowed with delight over a tree or a gate, all landmarks she guessed that measured the mile more surely than yards or feet. The youngest child had been left back at the house; without him all the others seemed all of a sudden older, as though his absence obscured some beginning, made all their separate origins, in infancy, a mystery. They were children with scarred knees and old towels over their shoulders.

'Can you swim at all?'

It was the man Colin, his dark eyes looking at hers. Am I a child or not she thought, watching her feet, white in their sandals, moving through the dust of the road. His feet were browned and ancient like the rocks left behind by the tide. What sort of man would be happy looking after children, walking down to the beach with them every summer afternoon? She heard her own voice, answering saying something about never living near the sea. A child had, once, but not this self.

When the littler children were safely playing in a rock pool, gathering starfish together like wandering posies, he took her hand and led her to a calm part of the deeper pool. The sea was safe, rebelling with a slap beyond the rocks.

'You children practise diving. Don't splash Jess or she'll never learn.'

They laughed, faces gleaming.

'First of all, learn to float otherwise you'll never trust the water.' She had never noticed his voice before.

The water was warm and still. But even now she could not believe that it would support her. How could her whole body, her feet and legs, not need the sand or rocks. She twisted on one foot watching the fumes of sand curl around her toes.

'All right then. Hold on to the rocks on either side. Lie like a star.'

She lay back feeling the water circle her head and silence her ears. Under her back she felt his hand lift her up until her body surfaced. It wouldn't work. She would sink.

But all of a sudden she saw the sky above, blue and burnt, and saw that he had moved away. She was alone, a star in a warm sky.

'Don't move, don't panic. Just let go of the rocks,' he said beginning to smile.

She felt the rock and then felt the sea beneath her as calm and even as a bed that might let you dream. One by one she let her fingers begin to trust the water not the rock. And you don't sink, you don't drown she thought, away in a different world. She touched the rock, and this time in all the wonder of knowing she could drift, pushed herself away.

Burying her face in the clean washing a few weeks later Jessie thought about the last card she had received from Stephen, two months ago.

Dear Jess

How do you like being a working girl? There's not much

doing here anymore. I've seen a bit of the West and I intend looking for work in the city again after Christmas.

Cheerio,
Stephen

His messages were always so brief. And yet you could take a long time over the card, look at the picture on the other side (it was usually of a beach, in black and white) and wonder, desolate, all of a sudden, whether Stephen had actually walked on that jetty or sat by himself, or with someone, on that beach. She still always wrote back to him, long descriptive letters. The Misses approved, and had them posted.

She went on taking the washing off, shaking out creases so that the cloth jumped away from her hands, obedient and docile. She could fold the sky with those hands. All of a sudden Victor tripped and fell over the prop that she had put against the fence when she lowered the line.

'Oh Victor, Victor.' She rushed to the squalling boy and held him to her chest covering the little bump on his forehead with kisses and shutting her eyes against the sweet smell of his skin. His tears tasted like the sea in her mouth. And suddenly she was close to tears herself, not just because he was hurt and hot and crying in her arms. Some unhappiness had sulked on the edges of her life for weeks and now it came stalking into the open, at last admitted, tooth and claw.

She tried to gain delight from Victor's soft fluttering kisses. 'What sort of kisses do you like best?' They sat on the cane chair on the side verandah. The little boy squirmed in her lap. To choose.

'Fishes' kisses, eskimo kisses or ordinary kisses?'

'Jus' kisses.'

Her pay had increased. She was grown-up. Fifteen years old and allowed to cut off her plaits: is that what it meant?

'I'm writing to Miss Symes, to tell her how pleased I am with you.'

If I had six children, she thought, walking back to the kitchen, carrying Victor, though he wriggled to walk, would I still be as pretty as Mrs Gerard.

Stephen, she suspected had almost forgotten about her. He hadn't written for months.

She was allowed walks. They were healthy. The walk along the cliff top gave you choices. You set out from the house as if going to the beach, passing through the wormwood hedge that limped up the hill, all lumps and straggling, hardly a hedge at all. From here, before you dropped down the hill to the main road, you were poised on one side of the valley. Sometimes she thought if you could fly, this would be the point from which to push off, toes hard into the ground and up into dreams. But to get to the cliffs you had first to descend down the dusty road to the beach.

She always decided before she left the house. A mood of irritation would refuse to leave, buzzing inside her head with the dull pain of a wasp under glass. Then she would walk angrily down to the dusty road, feeling the few little houses staring at her itching back from behind their glaucous curtains. When she wanted the walk on the cliff top she could ignore the sea. But the sand would stretch before her, the first obstacle. You just had to plod through it, slipping and squeaking, every step making you feel more and more off balance, defining your feet as lead.

The second obstacle was the creek. You could walk along it, down the sand to the sea and there, when it ceased to be a creek and became a hand of water, fingers touching the sea, you could walk across, one eye on the waves, shoes hardly wet. Today she ran at the bank and leapt, feeling her hat halo behind on its ribbons, tight against her neck. On the sand cliff of the creek's edge she left a landslide but her feet were dry and she had crossed.

Now the cliff stood in front of her, the dun and dirt side of Lion's Head, a rocky scramble up the track that dithered among the gorse, a stunted path where sheep might scrape and slide to the fatter grass below. She legged upwards, determined not to stop. She would not look back until she reached the end. Her heart began to knock, asking for rest, but she would, she would push on until she could climb no more.

The top and she was there. The wind took her like a straw in its teeth, chewing her clothes and worrying its grey voice in her hair. She was a mast flapping flags, a snag in the river's flow. Turn around and you could see the little town clinging to the slope on the far side of the creek. None of the houses ventured up onto the plains that stretched to the kingdom of the hills; they huddled in the broken green of the valley.

Up here she had choices. She might walk north for mile after mile, watching the sea crawling below, her eyes knowing no boundaries. There would be nothing above but the desolate sky, beneath her striding feet the hurried grass. Her eyes could take on the bold stare of the eagle, the giant's gaze. The world would fall beneath her flight. Some days she could choose to descend, disappear off this stage, by any one of a dozen secret paths to the cave of air, the secret stillness of Chinaman's Cove. But today she would stay on top of the cliff, the smell of salt and earth enough.

On the way up the headland her body had been wooden. But here on the cliff top you could run or shout, smoulder into the satisfaction of flames, a fire-stick whirring in the wind's quivering palms.

In the little sitting-room, curtained against the darkness and the wind, the three women sat in the evening under the light.

Miss Amelia was being fitted for a cardigan. Jessie, sitting in the corner of the room, looked up from the radio and watched as Miss Edith held the cardigan across her back. The cardigan was sea-green with fussy detail around the neck. In it Miss Amelia would become some sea creature, remote and beautiful, her eyes the colour of the jumper. She turned now, to look over her bony shoulder at Miss Edith, who was trying to flatten out the knitting at the edges.

'It won't be long enough, I don't think Edith.'

'It's what the pattern says.' There was a silence. Miss Edith pulled and stretched the cardigan at the shoulders. Miss Amelia's red hair looked dark and glowing in the light. Her pale face set, as rocks might pull under the sand at the tide's retreat.

Miss Edith took the knitting and sat down in her chair as though she were alone in the room, even the world. You might turn away to the radio again or watch for the next move. Of course Miss Amelia came and sat next to her sister on the sofa.

'Edith.' It was her soft voice. The other woman looked up from the pattern book and smiled. Impasse became reconciliation. You love it, Jessie thought. You would willingly unpick the shoulders of the cardigan, and knit more rows so that it fitted exactly as Amelia wanted. You love being so useful. She went on pretending to read the paper, half listening to the radio. Only the necessity of having to get up and make supper prevented her from approaching the abyss which threatened if she considered whether anyone had ever taken the measure of her shoulders and adjusted with love the work of their hands.

Where did it all begin she would ask herself later?

Standing with the Misses Wilson in the bare little churchyard near the school, feet on the gravel. Was it here perhaps? The church was a lofty freestone building set in a little fenced wilderness. Wild looking wind-blown shrubs passed for a garden. Around it, the few little streets of the hamlet and then the empty flatness of the plain, gold and grey, the hills behind, the sea hidden and distant. It was an autumn day, yet heat still hung in the air.

'One could wish that the brims of summer hats were what they used to be,' Miss Edith remarked.

Jessie remembered that, because her hat was old-fashioned and had a brim you could hide behind.

They were standing in a little group near the gate. Amelia Wilson was being talked at by several families at once. Miss Edith glanced in her direction. 'How tiring it must all be,' she said to Jessie. She moved slowly in towards her, rescue in mind. And then they were all in a group, Colin in his suit and she in hat, gloves and best dress, more strangers now than they had been, half naked on the beach.

This was not really where things began. You sat in church beside the Misses Wilson, impatient and bored, fiddling with your gloves. You had already thought about whether the new cotton you had on would wear well and whether your shoes would last another season. She glanced down at Miss Edith's shoes: they were of beautiful soft leather; she supposed she couldn't really ask where she bought them or how much they had cost. And then suddenly she was conscious of being observed. Colin was in the pew directly opposite hers and the small congregation was sitting still, supposedly listening to the sermon, so that she couldn't move or look, beyond darting a sideways glance.

The length of the sermon was something Jessie could never determine, yet today, it allowed her to cross and uncross her legs several times and straighten her gloves. She sat up straight at first and then, convinced all of a sudden, that she looked stiff, starched, she relaxed again. She wondered whether her elbows were clean, for the dress she was wearing had the new elbow-length sleeves, and then reflected that since he was not sitting behind her he wouldn't be able to see her elbows in any case.

The sermon finished. Jessie dropped onto the kneeler for the prayer and felt hot and uncomfortable. At the back of the church a baby began to cry, the sound wavering out like their thoughts, hopelessly, upwards to an uncaring god. Jessie could hear the mother try to quieten the sound, the shuffling and whispering. She carried it out and the door shut to silence again and the minister's even voice.

With a sense of relief, surely felt by even the most devout Jessie thought, everyone rose to sing the final hymn. Dresses became less damp as the hymn books were opened. One of the Gerard boys dropped his hymn book just as the singing commenced and in the little stir that this created Jessie was able to glance sideways. She met the eyes of the man who had watched her, a stranger, not the Colin she knew. As her head turned back to watch the minister, she was suddenly less conscious that Miss Edith, singing in her flat voice, had not noticed a thing, than she was of the bad impression that her impiety must create (for she was sure it was visible), and so she sang with grace and feeling, her head inclined at what she hoped was a graceful angle under the little hat, her hymn book held aloft in a serious manner, hands gloved against their trembling.

'This little port was named for an Aboriginal word meaning "birth of the wind",' Miss Edith said slowly into the silence.

They sat drinking tea on the front verandah. The afternoon was honey calm; nothing ruffled the lace curtains at the window. The palm tree on the edge of the garden held the sky, stained glass between lead fingers. Within the house everything stayed decorous and calm, unmoving in the hot air. The sun danced on the wood of the verandah and she longed to kick off her shoes, roughen her heels on that coarse grain, pad through the warmth. But that would never do. It would be inexplicable. Watching the shadow of a cloud pass across the golden hill on the other side of the valley, she heard

Edith Wilson make some remark about the trees or the hill, which was it, she thought after a moment?

She smiled her assent to the words.

Opposite the house, on the other side of the road, was an enormous two-storey hotel, long since shut up and vacant. The owners came down from the city only as often as was needed to keep it in perfect order so that it wouldn't attract men 'on the track', the Misses had told her. She liked it, she couldn't tell why, had grown already to love the sun and shadow on the biscuit of its walls. In the valley at the bottom of the hill, the creek hid in a dark green scribble of shrubs limping down to the sand in stagnant pools. Lion's Head edged the view, torn by the blunt scissors of the waves. From this verandah, if she turned her head she could see the far-off hills and valleys of McLaren Vale, lying distant and unvisited like another province, unreachable without stars and sails.

Today she watched the hill, enjoying the enormous wind shivers that ran across it now and now, again. A line of cows appeared and worked their way along the crest of the hill. They might have been set in motion by an artist she thought, so perfectly did they eat their way along the crest, lengthening their shadows step by slowing step. It was a scene of order: the golden hill, the silent building and the wind, reflected now for me she thought ruefully looking at her watch, only in the windows of the house. She turned to take in the tray.

Drying plates, several hours later, feeling how slowly the week was moving towards Sunday, she suddenly heard the wind that gave the little port its name come rustling through the dark towards the house. She had felt at home, once again hearing all day the distant turning and folding of the sea, but this wind that blew across the plain (only after the windows of the house were long since black), some nights with force and others with idleness, made her afraid. Putting the plates in the cupboard, she heard the timbers of the house creak against the flow. A window in the sun-room banged shut. All the curtains in the house shivered inside the shut panes. She hurried through the last few saucepans so that she could leave the scullery and go in and sit with the two ladies and put between herself and the wind's terror some simple activity, reading, knitting; a row, a page. In the distance she heard the sea.

Climbing into bed later that night she saw her own face in the mirror, serious and deep-eyed, to the wind's wild transformations, considering the storm.

When Colin smiled at Jessie she hardly knew what to do.

Of course her face and eyes smiled back but she was left with a feeling of utter confusion, of having nothing to give. She didn't know what to do with her hands.

They were standing in the churchyard near the gate, the Misses Wilson having stopped to talk to an acquaintance, Mr Fitchett, the man who fished from the beach and sold his fish in the district. He was a stout man with a tiny lively face and broad shoulders. His face was full of quickness and intelligence but his legs were thin and short, too small-looking to support such strong arms. The Misses Wilson looked down on him, talking pleasantly. The Gerards were nearby, trying to regroup the younger members of the family; there was a no-man's-land between the two parties and Colin had, now, crossed it with his casual step and easy words. He was talking about, of all things she thought in a daze, the sermon.

He was looking straight at her so that she had to drop her eyes, feeling that he saw her too clearly with his glance. Why should she all of a sudden feel prickles of embarrassment along her shoulders as though something had happened? It was as though she had done something wrong, as though she might have to face the Misses Wilson and be rebuked when they arrived home for lunch after church. Meanwhile she was having to cope with his conversation which she managed to do, in the main by smiling at his comments on the sermon. She realized afterwards, going over the scene in her mind for not the first time, that she had listened as little to his comments as she had to the sermon itself; during the former she had been thinking of his face and now she was watching it, too enchanted with his eyebrows and his voice to listen to his words.

But the smiles! What she was left with afterwards, during the drive home and the work of the following days, was the feeling that she could hardly bear her own burden of happiness, that she must keep it somehow, hide it, tie it down so that it did not show, so that no one else would see what was happening or see that her awkwardness with her hands was due not to any nervousness but simply to the feeling that she had received more than a blessing in that smile; something, some gift that she did not understand, an offering, that she could not begin to realize how she might carry away and keep, had unrolled at her feet.

8

It might be there between them, that feeling. On good days she was certain of it.

But nothing happened. She went on having her swimming lessons every evening of the summer. The water did not fail her and she soon grew confident. She could swim away from the children now, not with speed but certainly with strength. She learnt to dive, returning from the depths with sand clutched in triumphant hands.

I'm avoiding his eyes though, she thought.

They were standing in a line in the sea, heads of different heights, waist or chest deep in the swell, waiting for the seventh wave. She was not sure she believed in that. But the children all believed and stood jumping with excitement, willing to make some excuse, some allowance when the eighth and ninth waves began to disappear.

'We won't count those. They're just ripples.' Gwen shouted to Colin, wanting him in their world.

'How do you know you began counting at the right moment?' he said laughing. They were delighted, she saw, by this complication.

Jessie moved away, not really wanting to be part of it.

How social swimming could be in the season she thought.

For it was the school holidays and bright canvas lean-tos fluttered green and white striped on the sand, small in the distance, vast domestic worlds close at hand, giving everything a human perspective. Families sheltered in their shade. Toddlers played on sand-irritated mothers. Near the sea's edge a boy knelt on all fours, luring the tide into a trench, his back an altar for the sun.

And here in the sea she thought, why it's like a party. No one really swims. They just talk in groups, white bathing cap to green. Out of the corner of her eye she saw the Gerards talking to Amelia and Edith Wilson, two by two as though the sea was a table and they at bridge.

'Jessie,' Mrs Gerard called, 'take the children for a walk please. They're going blue.'

When they were all in a line walking along the beach she realised that he was there too and though she was determined not to look at him, taking the cold hands of the two littlest children in her own, she knew that he was looking at her, sideways.

She wanted then to look, remembering how the sun had folded itself into the skin around his eyes. But she looked away instead. They were walking to Gull Rock, the longest and best of all the walks. There was a point on this walk where you could always choose to go back or to go on; that was the moment when you reached Lion's Head. It lay across the beach, beyond the swimmers, beyond the creek, jutting black rocks out into the sea, cutting off the view of the beach beyond. To walk around Lion's Head at low tide was arduous; rocks marred the sand. To walk around at high tide was a children's adventure.

When they had leapt from rock to waiting rock, half seriously avoiding the tide, the longer beach stretched before them, the square point of Gull Rock a squat and distant tower on a stretch of deserted sand. Above them lay the cliffs with their clay skirts bordering the sand in crinoline folds.

'They still look a bit blue,' Colin murmured. They; and that meant she was not, as he was not, a child.

'Race you,' he said to Gwen. 'Race all of you.' They broke into a dance in and out of the sand's gleam and she was surprised at her heart, fledgling to flight as she could at last, unseen, watch him laugh.

On the southern end of the beach was a jetty. It was a different walk, one to take in the late afternoon when the sun was warm on your shoulders and the sea, tired by a day spent arguing the toss limped towards the beach, abashed, ashamed.

She walked away from the clusters of families on the sand, feeling the sun beating upon her face as though she had just left the city walls and must rely upon herself in that golden loveliness until she reached Africa, somewhere the other side of all this airy heat, this world of sun she walked to cross.

There were no choices on this walk. It was the way she always took when she had to feel at home with the narrowness of things. You followed the sea's edge and in the end, an hour later, you reached the reef, sharp and harsh to the feet, a rocky wilderness she never liked. Beyond the reef was another beach, Aldinga, flat sand with no cliffs and no rocks, a landscape without memory or passage whose bleak continuities she had seen once. That was enough.

You walked south on the sea's edge to the jetty. It was unsafe, destined to become a ruin in twenty years, tall timbers standing like tide markers far out among the waves. Under the jetty she paused, trapped by the smell and sense, the sea's concentrated breath. Every wave and every tide had left its mark, one by one on this wood. Trees that had grown far from salt water had been so often waist deep, prisoners in the surf that they had grown to resemble their prison; weathered, bleached, between the lines of their old skin, the hardest of snails.

Beyond the jetty the beach turned, curtseyed its waves into a little bay where it was safe to swim. If you looked back here you would see a road cut through the cliffs to the jetty, a walled corridor of stone for carts of slate from the hills beyond the plain. She never walked back along this road. It was steep. Clay peaks on either side blocked the pleasures of sighting either sea or hills and she hated climbing among all that barren dirt, the silence of pebbles and dust.

So she kept on walking, the wall of cliffs on one side, the sea on the other, the sand beneath her feet becoming with every turn and twist, a narrowing path. On this walk you could hardly ever be alone in the summer. You were bound to pass someone or overtake someone and on that narrowing path it was uncivil, impossible not to nod or bow.

Thus she saw him a long way off on the edge of the reef and knew that he had seen her and that she would have to talk. There was no escape except to turn back and that would be evasion not escape.

In the end the sea ran to meet the cliff, the sand, washed flat, gave way to the stone crests of the reef. She watched him walking towards her across the vast empty flatness. He picked his way past pools and rocks not looking at her. The reef was as flat as the sea beyond; brown rock to the horizon.

She stayed near the cliff.

'It's impossible to walk on this rock,' she said by way of apology. Her bare toe gestured at the sharp stony crust from where she stood.

'That's not rock.'

She looked at him and then back down at the dry deadness, the city of little cones.

'They're barnacles,' he said.

How can they live she wondered. Each one looked dead, a husk of dry stone, a rounded shadow against the heat.

'Ah well,' he said standing very close to her as they began

to walk back on the narrow sand, 'some things can survive on occasional high tides; they just have to wait.'

'You can ask them for me. Whether they want an Easter bird as usual.'

She had seen him coming to the door before he knocked, and in the moment before her heart began beating in her chest in a way she felt was ridiculous, she had a moment of disbelief when she did not realize it was he at all, but one of the Gerard boys or perhaps Mr Gerard himself.

She stood at the door, half laughing. Not a romantic opening line she thought but then her face became serious because he was not smiling, not smiling at all. She noticed in the confusion two details, that he smoked a pipe and that he was not young. Then she went inside to the sitting-room to ask. It appeared that a chook was required, so she walked to the back door wishing she could think of something light to say.

He had turned away and was stroking the cat. She walked out to where he was squatting on the ground.

'They do want one, thanks.' He looked at her from where he was, embarrassing her as much by looking up as when he had looked down at her from the doorway.

'And how do you like working for the Misses?'

She looked back down the hill at the little house and then at Colin. He had guessed already she saw, before she even opened her mouth; his own face and eyes were a mirror for her own wry mouth.

'I'm in the same boat,' he said as they reached the top of the garden.

'But the Gerards – they're your family!'

'That's why they keep me on. They don't need me. Two years of bad harvests and I'm an expense.'

She looked down at the roof of the house; her place. Beyond

it stretched the golden hills and somewhere miles beyond that lay the city. She couldn't think what to say.

'I failed after the war; on my own block.' He was looking at her now with some plea in his eyes. They stopped. She would have to go back. But she looked at him and found her gaze, steady and forgiving, as much wonder as comprehension, fitted perfectly, and slid in his sight, she realized in bewilderment, like a key in a lock.

'That Easter bird was delicious.'

Mrs Gerard looked pleased; the hens were her province.

'They benefit from a scratch, I think,' Miss Amelia contributed.

Jessie went on sewing, sitting on the back verandah steps of the Gerard's house, repairing a cuff, her thread going up and down in the clear light.

The back verandah of the Gerard's house happily faced the sun and the whole lovely valley that ran down to the sea. A house full of rooms and children, that's heaven, Jessie thought dreamily as she went to the bright square of light that was the back door. But he wasn't there.

They began afternoon tea. The older Gerards and a frail aunt sat on the verandah in the shade, the six children tumbled down the lawn, discs of falling colour against the green, the whole valley yellow beyond them in the sun.

'Cup of tea?'

'Love one, thanks.'

That voice and no other. His hair was freshly washed and dark with water. He sat down on the verandah steps and watched her sewing, the tea-cup in his hand. Straight away Jessie felt tight with shyness.

After one quick look she bent her head over her sewing again. What was she thinking as her needle went up and down? He followed the needle and thread with his eyes, not ceasing to watch her face, his own smiling and intent, the tea growing cold in his hand.

'Are you warm enough?'

With a start Jessie realized Colin was speaking to her. She looked up, caught his glance and realized she could not say the 'yes' that had sprung, untruthfully, to mind.

'No I'm not really,' she smiled, hearing her own voice graceless after his low one.

He went inside.

All the Gerards bore a strong resemblance to each other except Colin, she realized with a shock, as she went up to replace her cup on the tray. They all had high square foreheads, coloured by the sun, and blond curly hair, woolly, without shine. Colin was younger than his brother, but his forehead was more creased, his eyes more surrounded by lines.

Something had marked his face, the same thing that had turned his hair to ashes, before the flames had died in his eyes. Seeing all the complications too clearly she thought suddenly. It was a face without colour, everything was etched, everything spoke with the directness of black and white.

She sat down again on the steps and picked up her sewing. Above her in the shade of the verandah Mr Gerard was gazing ruminatively at the valley, detaching himself with heavy grace from the women on the other side of the table who were discussing the children's health. At the end of the garden the children were shrieking and wrestling on the lawn.

The door banged and Colin walked out past his brother's quick glance to where Jessie sat. He was carrying a rug made of bright Afghan squares. It was not the first time anyone had ever asked if Jessie were cold, and it was not even the first time she had felt loved; on reflection, to balance these moments when she felt most alone she had decided she had been tolerably well loved, off and on, even if a great amount of the time she had been dependent on letters or infrequent meetings for her happiness, but she knew with a sense of fatal shock that no one she had known had ever put a rug around her shoulders with such tender decisiveness, with a gesture that let the gaudy wool fold around her like another's arms so that she raised her face, startled, as if he had touched her.

It seemed, after that, that there could be nothing to be afraid of and Jessie felt herself meeting his gaze as easily as a swimmer rises up from drowning and breaks through the rocking, silver flatness of the surface, to breathe, to live. There seemed to be nothing between their faces or their eyes, no need to talk and only a thousand familiar pleasures in the other's glance. The rest of the party, all around them, talking and eating might not be there, so far away did they seem, Jessie thought calmly.

She went on sewing as if dreaming, lost to the past or the future, intent upon the rolled seam but more aware with every minute of the very absence of any barriers between them, in the absolute rightness of their being so apart and so close as they sat amongst all those others, not talking, not even, any more, smiling at each other, but each aware of the other with more certainty than if they had been dancing, holding each other, face to face, the thread with every movement, shortening in her hand.

That autumn the creek flooded.

She was not surprised. All through the night she had heard the rain driving on the roof of the house, falling around the windows like curtains between the night and the glass. Her nights were never free of dreams and wakefulness and every time she awoke, walking out of some dimly lit scene of menace or pleasure, she would hear the neutral sound of the rain falling as though it were part of the darkness, enduring with the stars till morning.

At the Gerards there was a sense of excitement. Gwen must see the creek.

Jessie left the house with Gwen, who was delighted by her

long boots. The baby toddled to the door and cried and watched them walk down across the lawn. In the garden, rhododendrons sheltered under the drooping prunus, chickens under a dripping wing. The flood encompassed everything. Trees appeared in its skirts, wallflowers in a dancing lake. The two girls stood right at the edge.

In the distance Jessie could see a new river making its way on top of the lake where the creek usually ran its lazy course. Sticks and branches were bowled along, snagged and then broke free. Holding Gwen's hand, Jessie turned and looked back at the house. How small it looked at this distance, like some boat moored above the tide. The house was cut off by this flood from the city. Water had covered the little low bridge on the main road.

She felt her eyes go out of focus.

Where was she? She wanted to stop and consider it all; herself, Colin, the changes of the past three months. They had begun as strangers and what were they now? They were not lovers. And yet without that word she could think of no way to describe the way she had travelled. Without that word there could be no understanding of my every moment. Night and day, but that was only a song.

Looking down at her feet, she saw small insects frantically clinging to tall blades of grass. Some fell off but others managed to cling on despite the waves that kept shaking their safety.

They were so modern. And yet she did not eat with them.

In a way she liked sitting in the kitchen alone, eating without pretence. Certain they would not approve, but liking the companionship of his name on the outside of the letter, she used the time to write to Stephen, a word between each slice, each bite. He had been working in the West. She wanted him to come and see her now he was back in the city. Perhaps he might not have changed but she wanted to watch his face, to see in his eyes some recognition of what he must see was different in her. She put down her pen. She couldn't write about Colin but of course when Stephen came they would meet. They would like each other I'm certain, she thought.

There was a knock.

'There's a man at the door who wants a bit of food, Ma'am.' Jessie stood uncertainly at the door of the dining-room.

'Tell him to keep moving Jessie,' Miss Edith said. Jessie frowned and went out. The man looked tired and dirty. His teeth were yellow, she saw from the top of the steps.

'I'm sorry,' Jessie said, 'the mistress says you're to keep moving.'

'I'm a returned man Miss,' he said, the depths of his degradation reached. Jessie paused and went back to the dining-room.

'Excuse me. He says he's a returned man.' Miss Amelia hesitated, her spoon in mid-air. Miss Edith looked up from her soup, annoyed.

'You can still tell him to keep moving Jessie. We can't feed them all. He'll probably get something in the town.'

In the ways she loved most, Stephen had not changed.

'Two years in the West. What can I say? I worked in the mining towns, on a farm, in a warehouse. It was near the end of me sometimes. It's terribly difficult finding work when there are more and more blokes losing their jobs.'

'I'm finished Jess,' he said without anger, throwing a clod of earth into the slowly moving waters of the receding creek. How could that face beneath his greasy hat look so sharp and lined? She watched him put his hand in his pocket as they walked, hating the way the threadbare cuffs on his trousers were becoming dusty from the earth.

They came to a bend in the river that almost enclosed an island. 'Skeleton Grove', the children had called it. It was full of dead thistles, waist-high, a field of husks, stalks as high as a man. Stephen walked among the grey and white forest breaking a path through the whole field of whispering sceptres, but she knew they would only come to the creek again, too deep to wade across.

Walking back on the same path he mentioned a name, Pamela.

'I've left her in Perth. She's better off without me.'

She stopped and looked up at him. Was that true, she wondered.

'We knocked about a bit. She's in the family way now.' No wonder all his messages on the backs of post-cards had been so brief.

'A baby?'

'Of course, you silly thing. She says she'll come over here to live. You'd like her. She's a good sort. Likes a beer, likes a bet. But only a zac each way.' It was like drinking from a glass and cutting your lip on a crack, to hear the admiration in his voice.

'Will you get married?'

'She'll marry me, no doubt about it.' But you, what do you want, she thought.

Out loud she said 'I suppose I'm being naive.'

He laughed at her kindly and they set off back to the house.

'Madam's a right queen' he said presently, jerking his head at the house. They had not talked about the Gerards.

'She's all right,' Jessie said surprised.

'She's the Chief Puppeteer.' There was a silence.

She had never thought of the family like that. 'I quite like them.'

'Look, you work for them. Get the most out of it and clear out.'

But of course he had not met Colin.

'I thought we might try swimming out to the wreck, one fine day soon.'

They were walking on the beach towards Lion's Head, Jessie,

Colin and Stephen. She glanced at Stephen. Of course they had only just met, the two men, but already she was desperate to ask Stephen what he thought.

'Can you swim Stephen?' Colin asked. Why did she feel he was being so friendly?

'Of course.'

They walked around the headland and up amongst the rocks.

'There.' Colin pointed from where they sat. 'You can usually see it at low tide.'

She looked along his arm down the sand out onto the smooth blue of the sea. If he hadn't told her she would have thought that black triangle the cruising fin of a porpoise or shark and expecting it to move or disappear would have made it do so by moving her forgetting eyes. But sitting here with her hands cupped around her face she saw it pause and stay above the streaming waves, a topmast of a drowned ship, the memorial to all that rope and sail.

'Forty years ago,' Colin said. There was a silence.

She thought of the sudden scrape of timber on rock, the sea no longer a cradle but a jaw, grinding everything to sand, grain by grain.

'Are we going to sit here all day?' Stephen was getting up.

The next afternoon, her hair still wet from the swim, she challenged him about it.

'We were half way there. I thought you were just behind us. And I look back and you're walking back along the beach.'

It had begun wonderfully. In all the calm sunniness of the morning he had run past them and splashed head first under the waves. Even Colin had smiled. He looks like a boy, she thought laughing, watching him beating his arms into the surf, all blond bravery.

She and Colin and Walter Gerard had walked slowly behind

154

him, feeling the water's cold power.

'This is sort of like your reward Jess,' Walter said shyly.

They swam slowly out, watching the mast of the ship ahead of them like another swimmer. She had been out of her depth many times but had never swum out and out like this, feeling the sea fathoms deep beneath her feet as though she were weightless, a butterfly that might sink into the wet meadows of the sea.

Only then did she look back. He was walking back to the house. The others had already noticed but were too kind to say anything.

'They thought you'd chickened out.'

'Who gives a damn what they think. I just didn't want to.'

To add to the taut horrible moment, she was afraid that Miss Edith would walk into the kitchen. It should have been marvellous; his visit, his standing here in the kitchen with her after two years absence. But he was angry with her.

'You'd do anything he suggests, wouldn't you,' he said quietly, standing close to her as she stirred the soup.

'I quite like him,' she said carefully.

'I reckon myself, he's a bit odd.' He walked away to the window and stood looking out at the grassy rise.

'What a sleepy dump this place is. As soon as I set up in the city, come and live with us Jess. We'll have some good times.'

He was generous and it was what she most wanted to hear. Why then were his words so painful? She turned away, thinking of the wreck in all those fathoms of water, the wooden ribs they had glimpsed far below fleshed with sand, herself floating above it in trusting delight.

'These latest figures.'

'They should do something.'

'What?'

Jessie carried in the corned beef and set it carefully in front of Miss Amelia. It wouldn't do to spill meat juice on that white cloth.

'Simmons, Bill Simmon's father, that is, was laid off last week.' Miss Amelia cut four thick slices for Jessie and then began the slow, fine slicing for her sister.

'There must be something – '

'My dear where?'

Jessie carried her plate out to the kitchen. In the other room she heard the discussion continue. Amelia Wilson was telling her sister about the children at her school whose fathers were out of work. Edith considers her sister an authority on everything Jessie recognized, because she speaks with such confidence and force. Often when she was carrying the dishes to and fro, she would hear Amelia convince Edith by some long terrible story. It was serious dinner-time conversation. Between them, the sisters would sift through the explanations that were offered at length in the daily paper for the thousands unemployed. But I know how it will end, Jessie thought. Edith will glance at Amelia's half-finished meal and say, 'Don't let it get cold dear.'

Jessie had been dreaming and awoke in the still of the night after the wind had dropped, feeling the warmth of the dream. The house was very silent. She had never dreamt about Colin before.

In the dream they had walked into the sea and it had been calm and flat and green. He had stood next to her and put her forearm under the surface so that she could see the tiny silver bubbles caught by the golden hair on her arm. It had been done with the gentleness with which he did everything. They had stood together in the flat wide sea, his hand on her arm and the gesture alone was so deliberate and intense that she had been as aware of the vastness of the sea all around them and the flat calm of the early morning sky, as of him. Why did she love him? She could not have said, but the dream had been about that love, so that the simple gesture of holding her arm under the water had been charged.

She had known herself so at peace that her ears seemed to hear not only the impending breath of the smallest waves, but the sound of their breaking on the sand, all the way along the distance of the beach, and at the same time, she had heard the tiniest noises of the land behind the sea, the small cries of birds above the cliffs and the sound of sheep somewhere inland. She could see the colours of the sea, pale green and dully reflecting, for the first time, as if she stood on the edge of the sea but knew about it where it was deep and dark and could now see new colours that before, had passed unnoticed. In the dream she knew the landscape of the yellow and green cliffs and the confusion of the rocky headlands in a way that was entire and complete, so that if she had looked down on it from some great height there would have been nothing to surprise her, nothing she would have, on close examination, found inexplicable because, with her arm held under the sea by his, she sensed that in their contact, there was, for both of them, a realization that made all other things, in that moment when she saw the silver bubbles rise towards the surface of the water, ephemeral and unimportant.

'We'll never be able to marry you know.'

Did he want to dissuade her, she wondered. They were walking down to the beach through the warmth of the summer night. Ahead of them the track cut down to the sea, a sea like some invisible beast, half asleep, turning over out of sight, reminding you of its power.

'How do you know so certainly that things won't change?'

They had their arms around each others waist and stopped in unison like dancers. She felt him sigh.

'They won't,' he said. 'We're too far away and anyway it's the same everywhere, this depression. Fools like us'll stay poor.'

She didn't feel poor just then, stepping into the sand in the dark.

'I wonder why no one's seen the change in me. It's your doing you know.'

'They probably think it's the sea air, or the swimming,' he teased, kissing her hair and neck, having to stop because she had stopped, toes curled into the sand to kiss him properly.

'You promised to show me the phenomenon of phosphorescence,' she said, imitating his voice when they finally arrived at the sea. He was laughing and soft-voiced.

'There.'

He bent and raked the edge of the surf with his fingers.

She saw the tiny sparks of light, brief lives in the night. The sea rushed in wet ropes around their feet. Her shoes were left behind in the house; ordered under her bed, dancing red shoes defying the pastoral oversight of the Misses Amelia and Edith, allowing her in bare warm feet to slip away, to make love to this man, head to toe, her arms around his neck.

He walked them into the dunes away from the sea and he lit a fire despite her fears that it would be a beacon, a lighthouse that would turn the two foolish sisters into witches, harpies who could find her out and destroy. She watched his face and sometimes she forgot to talk or answer because there was such a delight in seeing the lines around his mouth come and go, woven into smiling.

'They won't wake, don't think of it,' he said when the fire caught.

He came and sat next to her, but it was she in the end who reached over and put her arms around his neck locking them, feeling as though her whole body must fall towards his, her breasts the perfect heavy blossom for the calyx of his fingers.

The house that Charles Wilson had designed for his daughters in the little port was built on a hill so that while the front looked out to a 'view', the back looked out to the hill itself, the front of the house inviting contemplation and repose; the back, domesticity and usefulness. Jessie, ironing in the kitchen one Tuesday afternoon, found herself staring out through the windows at the slate path, the geraniums and the almond trees. The iron was reheating on the stove and Jessie was thinking, as she nearly always found herself these days, about Colin. Considerable time and ingenuity went into devising situations where she and Colin could meet without being discovered. To the small township (and Edith and Amelia Wilson), they were in the early and public stages of a formal courtship and to maintain this artifice required elaborate preparation.

Running the iron carefully down an embroidered pillow-case, enjoying the smoothness left in the iron's wake, Jessie thought with desire of her afternoon walks.

Wednesday afternoons off began, she had long ago found out, no earlier than 2 p.m. She was permitted then to walk carefully about the streets of the little port with the respectable Colin Gerard. They were not permitted to walk on the beach and to avoid suspicion, did not do so. They would be farewelled by Miss Edith, who would also ask, in a very direct way when they returned, as if it were a matter of no consequence and she not a person with any authority over Jessie, where they had walked.

For Colin and Jessie being able to walk together was a pleasure. I'm gay and he's thoughtful she realized; each found in the other a complement. But because our walks are a façade they are more than a pleasure. If they set off up the steep little road that led past the side of the house they would begin to talk the moment they were out of earshot and they usually talked all the way along the road until the bay suddenly appeared far below to their right. But in their talking and the way they walked, if it was Colin slashing at the grass with a stick or Jessie finding a stone in her shoe, a slow tension would grow up between them. Walking out together under the eyes of the few townsfolk they met, having to be in each other's company and yet be prevented from touching or kissing meant that their walks became a series of slow, secret aches that they expressed perfectly in a glance as they returned down the road to the Misses Wilson. Their walks through the town every Wednesday afternoon, reserved, controlled, apart, became part of their being lovers in the dunes at night; a symmetry of postponement and consummation that mocked the iron bars of convention and control.

When Amelia Wilson's school had a 'Continental' to raise funds to purchase a radio for the school, Jessie with her two excellent chaperones helped Mrs Gerard set out chairs around the edge of the school hall. The people of the district, clustering around the stalls outside in the grassy paddock between the hall and the school, waited for the dance, hot and restricted in their best. The hall was large and seldom used, in its dusty spaces motes of sound lingered in their fall. Around the door, someone had draped streamers, their primary colours bright against the dull wood. It was still light outside, but the sun had gone, and the high windows of the plain little hall propped opened against the heat caught on their glassy grime the earliest stars.

A middle-aged man with a trumpet, his wife who played the piano and a youth who played the mouth organ had just begun when Jessie saw the Gerard family arrive and Colin's smile. He came over to chat politely to Jessie and Edith.

'It's the sound of poverty, the mouth organ. Poor man's music,' he said when they were left alone. She stopped, staring into his eyes as the threadbare sound rubbed at the timber walls.

No one was dancing except a few school girls in short frocks and white socks, dancing with each other and amusing their younger brothers. Later the hall became crowded. Jessie and Colin had decided, days before, that they would dance infrequently with each other so while Colin, tanned and thin in the suit he wore to church, danced with Miss Amelia, whose duties in making the evening a success seemed to have, at last, finished, Jessie danced with Bill Gerard. Bill was fourteen and as nervous as one can be, who, first in long trousers, attempts to cross the barrier that divides children dancing from the unattainable mysteries of grown-ups dancing together. He was falling at that moment between two different desires: a wish that the dance was over and he back with the children on the seats near the stage and an impulse to pay his small bright dancing partner with her yellow frock and easy ways, some unforgettable compliment.

All that Jessie looked forward to from the evening was the peace, the ease, after being handled by awkward youths and red-faced farmers, of dancing with Colin, whose hands and every movement seemed as familiar and tender as her own body.

'What is it?' she asked of the music as they danced at the edge of the tired crowd.

'It's just a love song,' he said.

He looked down at her disappointed face. 'I can't remember the words. It couldn't begin to say what I feel, what I'd want to tell you.'

She caught her breath.

'Why don't we tell everyone?' she asked.

He steered them into the centre of the floor. 'Because they could take it away from us,' he said flatly. 'From both of us – everything.'

How could you become locked in such an extremity of emotion? She felt buffeted, blown, beaten away from the sea, right to the edge, unable to begin to resist any of the flow of feeling, stunned by her loss of self: water washed far away, not only swept from the central calm but thrown beyond the utmost of the storm, tossed right across the rising waves, through and over their frothy heads across and beyond the rocks, far above the tide's tread to a sun-baked, landlocked pool, hot and contained beyond the firing of the waves; motionless, warm, enclosed. She lay, her head on one side on the pillow gazing into the dimness of his room, Colin's head on her cheek, her arms around his thin shoulders and then curved back to her body's beached arc.

That first time, so many months ago, she had expected pain and shock; as when sewing without a thimble, the blunt end of the needle forced back into your finger, the puncture of flesh, the shock of blood. But it had not been like that at all. And now. How could you describe that treasure.

'There are times,' she said, 'when I can hardly bear to look at you. When you look at me – ' She stopped. 'When you look at me I feel beautiful.'

He began to laugh so that she felt her stomach slapped by his. She drew back a hand and ran it in a zigzag she had learnt from the freckle on his cheekbone to his jaw and then next to his mouth.

'And I know I'm not.'

He looked at her, amazed.

'You're a nice girl,' he said, puzzled. 'But when you're undressed, when you take off your frock, your shoes and socks, your petticoat, your knickers, your camisole,' he paused, 'why, you're a dream, a smooth perfection in the flesh.'

There was a long silence. She was thought to be out for a walk. The Gerards were away at a wedding for a day, the house shut up against the heat, was his. Neither of us cares she thought suddenly. I don't care if he thinks I'm beautiful or not. She knew with the strength of the moment that she would never love anyone else, that she would never leave him.

'I don't understand.'

'What?'

'I mean it.'

'I wouldn't let it worry you,' he said so seriously that they both began to laugh.

Asleep in her arms he lay sprawled across the bed, his body quiet and unobserved. Asleep you could look at someone else, she thought, in a way you never could when they were awake. Usually she would catch a glimpse of him when they undressed, but then he was eager, aroused, shy, his cock already springing, loosed from clothes. And she was too smiling, her arms folded behind her head or out-stretched to give his body more than a glance, so that her eyes retained a quick sketch, a few brush strokes, not a shaded measured impression awash with colour and infused with light, but merely a part, perhaps his hard bottom, round under his shirt-tails. She turned to look at him. Asleep, his genitals lay innocent and small like round black-haired poppy buds, not curious or searching, immune she supposed, since they had already made love, to her own body's warmth. And perhaps even to her finger's touch.

His room was small and dark with a little verandah over the window to keep out the sun but between the bottom of the blind and the sill she could see the flat golden expanse of the summer wheat on the plain.

The house was silent. Her hand closed on him with a gentle brush like the tendrils of a vine. His cock felt like a sleeping bird in her hand; wrinkled and tender, his flesh stirred and crept inside the glove of her exploring palm. He started and curled towards her and her hand she felt him move and stretch like some creature that tenses, starts, sensing guns and game. She felt him change and grow, his cock easing itself inside her hand, in retreat and advance. Wanting more than anything in the heat and stillness of the room, on the narrow crumpled bed to hear him groan and gasp, she moved towards him, knowing what her hand was about and that it was the reason he moved towards her, his body now asking questions of its own.

They walked together after church to the far end of the walled garden cherishing the moments they could have together. They had been lovers for a year. And the pleasure does not lessen, she thought.

Behind them the congregation was still leaving. She looked back. Miss Amelia had forgotten her gloves in the heat of her devotions, and was walking back towards the church door. She opened it with a reverential push. Perhaps they have fallen under the pews Jessie thought, then we'll have ten or more minutes together. She watched as the glass door swung open, Miss Amelia's entry catching the light on the glass and throwing it out to the worldly who talked around the steps.

She and Colin had very little to say. It had been a discovery, how well he understood her glance, the nuances of her mouth. Stephen had been like that. She never thought of him these days. Pamela had written, long ago, to say they had a daughter and were married and living in the city.

Colin clung on at the Gerards. One day they too would marry. She was certain.

They leant over the wall and looked at the neat rows of old stones, each with its dated summary of a life. These two things, birth and death, were so unplanned she thought. What made life good or bad between those dates? Was a long life any better than a shorter one? She thought of the Misses, of Miss Amelia on her knees searching for her gloves. That would be lunch-time conversation for them she thought, that's the staple of their frozen lives.

A butterfly had landed on her shoulder and now fluttered circling above her head. Her eyes followed and then went past its flight to the shock of seeing Colin's eyes had watched her every move, on his face the light she had seen a thousand times and saw each time as new.

'A room!'

'It's more than some have.'

He stopped and shook her by the shoulders, in pain not rage.

'I'm losing my job: all right. Young Bill's left school and he can do it. But you want us to set up like horses in a stall. That's not life. I'll be unemployed. Me and all the other thousands.'

Tears met in her eyes and she hoped he thought it the wind's doing not her own grief.

'There's rations. All right; the dole. Stephen says they get by.'

'Stephen says!'

He stopped and took her inside his coat, his arms against the wind.

'You go. I'll have to get a job somewhere. Maybe picking grapes on the river. When I get it, I'll write and you can join me.' In her tears there was still faith.

The depression will end she thought. I love him so much, even his weak shoulders, his slight frame. Surely he will get work. When this depression passes he will get a job in the city. Is it too much to want? To want not to have to choose between him and Stephen. That was what she wanted, she knew: the happiness of having them both close by, to be able to watch over them both. Why shouldn't she run at it, trying to take everything and catch it in her hands?

She left the little port, and waited for his letter, far away in the city.

9

Dress an elephant, she thought, deck it out in gaudy reds and set it parading, lifting up its belled trunk, and you would have this house, 'Montrose'.

As in any city, she discovered, here too, money ran uphill.

To the north of the planned city, inside the parklands, lay a special hill. The hill was a grid of streets, mean alleys without views but around the edges of the hill you could see forever. Here stood the tall two-storey houses within their own walled gardens, sequestered wealth. They ringed the hill like towers on a castle. From any one of these houses the city could be observed, at a distance, immense and proper, its roads and churches easily distinguished on a clear day, a summer's day.

A clear summer's day had ended and now the city was losing all the flat gold light; it fingered chimneys, slid down steeples and settled in the streets, pavement grey. Green and blue shadows lengthened on the blocks of buildings. Of all the castellated terraces of the suburb on the hill, the southern terrace, which overlooked the city, was the grandest, and of its houses, none could hold the light of a summer's evening as long as Montrose. It was not one of the older houses on the terrace and for this reason perhaps it was the most elaborate, with ornamental turrets and eaves and towers. It

166

commanded the corner of an important street so that anyone strolling on its wide verandahs could not only watch the parklands and, beyond them, the city, but also survey the two roads that trailed past outside the high freestone garden wall.

The verandahs of Montrose were paved with diamonds, red and black Italianate tiles. Trudging down the hill with the slow feet of one who has worked all day and only walks to save a fare, she could recall perfectly the pattern of the tiles; her rough hands proof that they were highly polished. She had polished them every week since beginning at Montrose. After all, everyone called, and these days, my dear, as Mrs Madingley had explained, some called without even telephoning first, although it was the height of rudeness and she really didn't know –

In the end you had to stop listening.

Today, as requested, at five, the modern cocktail hour, everyone had called. Such a crush! She could hear Mrs Madingley's voice. The cars parked in the streets for a block, the smart hard lipstick smiles behind short veils, the fashionable shapeless silk dresses, perfume and cigars, the tread of feet across the tiled verandahs, all this slipped behind, was over, thank goodness. The tiles would have to be repolished tomorrow. But now at least she was free and walking downhill from the suburb on the hill in the thick light of a summer's evening. She thought of that other self with an inner smile, that self who stood in a natty uniform, always polite, always smiling. She had stood handing around tray after tray of canapés with her practised and correct effacement whilst the high laughing buzz of conversation about the market, about Christmas parties, about parliamentarians (there had been a scandal) rose all around her. And to all those talking, chewing mouths she was merely the holder of trays, the stand for drinks or for empty glasses. No one met her eye. No one stopped for a second their unwise chatting. Words scraped out; toothpicks stuck to her ashtrays. You had to smile as if they were gifts.

From the bridge over the river she entered the city, losing any views, unable now to see its squareness and organisation, its churches and chapels. It was a place to forget yourself, a place where you could be alone, unknown and unbeckoned. You knew your way here, could walk it in your sleep, without defences. She took off her shoes and let them dangle from her hand.

Lights were just coming on, dimming the shabbiness, the cracked windows and peeling posters. A man and woman leant laughing, entwined, out of a hot small upstairs window. A piano tinkled, then stopped and a moment later, started again, as if, she mused, the player had paused to light a cigarette or simply leant back in his chair, balked by the heat.

Ignore you, she thought, seeing the lear of a man in braces who buttressed his door. Unpainted warehouses led to the humid shade of the square and four streets past the square, and there, at last was the alley off a side street. It was a brick-peeled cottage, one of a row of six. She pushed open the door and was home.

Sunday morning, peace. You awoke at ten to eight to the sounds of the city's churches calling the faithful to early morning communion. The middle room was dark and airless, one small window opening onto a space between houses. In the bed opposite, Marjorie, the eldest child of Stephen and Pamela, slept pressed against the wall in a twist of sheets that rocked silently on a quiet current. She had learnt to slide out of bed, leaving the child asleep. But today was Sunday.

On the back step she paused savouring the dust, the smells of summer off the boil. The leaves of the peach tree passed the sunlight, dribbling it from green palm to palm.

On the cracked step, suddenly there were the kittens, running about on clumsy legs, purring to her and her alone. She hadn't seen them for days. They rubbed her legs. Pamela had bought all three of them at a fête for a penny each. Why, there isn't enough food for us, Jessie had thought, seeing their heads bursting out of Pamela's coat-pocket like unruly flowers. But now she began to understand that Pamela had seen something else, something that only now appeared.

All human relationships were a tangle of kindness and hurt. Things might change but they would never resolve. Even a child soon began to be wilful. But the kittens were new delight. They fell over each other and rose up again, shameless in their admiration, clumsy on their trembling legs. A cat had a line of tension through its back, head to tail a drawstring of ease and energy that could be tightened in a moment's flash, clawed terror, rent prey. But the kittens had no tension, only pleas and pleasure, squeaking mouths.

Everyone betrayed you in the end. She walked into the staleness of the house. The kittens were innocent, new, with none of the world's hardness or hunt, cat's claw. She carved small fragments off the joint, dropping them in a shower onto their plates. Crusts of milk and gravy and bone chips circled each saucer, a primitive calendar, the record of a tribal life, hunger and harvest. Their world revolved around these saucers and they rushed and growled when she poured the milk. One kitten waded into the food. The smallest ate, vomited and ate in a short rhythm, shaking with excitement. She squatted down, her nightie sweeping the dust of the yard and satisfied their madness.

Out there in the city the bells called and called. It was months since she had been in a church. You fell away from it without a care. And then quite suddenly she thought of Colin. Usually her mind fluttered from thought to thought around the edges of that memory. That was where it had all begun, in a church. Salt, like the heavy air off the sea, splashed onto her wrists.

The kittens, artless in their need, were innocents in a world of snares. She cut squares of bread and dropped the morsels into their waiting mouths.

The little port where she had lived for years had begun to seem like another person's life. She wished those years would become a tiny thing, a distant view or one of those little paperweights filled with snow; nothing to do with the person she now was; something that could never hurt again.

And but for one thing, it might.

The person she was now slept in, talked late, drank cups of tea and gossiped. With Pamela and Stephen she had learnt to play cards, taking it as a new accomplishment. And then she realized. It was all a game. The moment they sat down around the table and Stephen began his one-handed, slick dealing, they all fell into roles as certainly and easily as the cards flew around the table into three heaps. These roles would never advance or retreat. Although each role allowed great variations in interpretation, space to overplay or understate, each knew the others' roles perfectly, they all knew exactly what to expect; like old actors performing a play for a provincial audience after months of touring, there would be nothing unexpected. The cards were the text: once they picked them up everything proceeded with pleasurable certainty. Pamela would not change from gently admonishing Stephen, from laughing, from knowing that her protests merely seemed to make Stephen more and more daring, Jessie would not change from being in a sense the closest to an audience, never interfering, just watching and laughing; they would always provoke each other, one by silence, one by words, so that the game played above the cards always lent itself not to intimacy or discovery but to pleasure for all of them, to certainty, no matter whose hand was favoured by the luck of the game.

Stephen's charm. Playing cards, talking around the table, sitting on the back step watching the children dig in the mean earth between the house and the shed; he was charming. To every encounter, with the children or us, with humorous quick glances, or a few spaced words, he brought his manner, such a lightness of contact that you felt enriched. He lives life in these moments, she thought; cruising along that changing line between himself and us. It's a tense energy that leaves nothing behind, no other considerations, no foresight, no responsibilities other than making the children shriek, or Pam and me smile delight.

She supposed this was abundance after years of post-cards. Somewhere at the back of a drawer they all lay, each one with a few sentences from Stephen on the back and a picture of some town or beach on the other side, not portraying at all how things really were in that little town – how could one card do that? – but showing one part of the town, a picturesque part with bright colours jostling to fit forms and sometimes overlapping slightly so that the poor little town might have one road stained purple and an orange-edged sky.

In the beginning she had written long letters to Colin thinking as she wrote them how he would read them, what they looked like as he drew them out of the envelope and how he might smile. Certain passages were written to do just that. She had hoped that he would write. The pain she felt after weeks of silence did not lessen.

She sat hunched over her letter, a word. Her own letters, from the heart, probably seemed wordy and childish. They might even bore the person he must have become. She began sending him instead, a few cheerful lines, with long spaces, weeks, between the words.

Now she knew she would have to stop writing. Long ago, she remembered Stephen saying what can letters tell.

She thought how careful he had been every time they made love. In the sun of midday a trail of ants would feast at the silver globules, dusted with sand and then creep back into the boobialla that clung as they did in the night to the sanctuary of the dunes. In a way it spoilt the ease and pleasure, his abrupt wrench from the fit of her own body, but how could they afford a child.

Dear Colin, she had written. She stopped. In front of her sat the pencil and paper, quite useless. She was alone at the kitchen table, Pamela having taken her children shopping. The open door showed her the bare space of the yard, the dust and curls of peach leaves, that short space, never room enough for the children to play or the washing to dry, all that they owned, all the space they had in the city of the poor. Somewhere out there with space to drift, space to linger, Colin walked free or so she might imagine in the long hours given to remembering him. But in her heart she knew it was not like that. He kept moving through the huge expanse of the state and around the corner, somewhere, might lie the fertile niche that could shelter tumbleweed from the wind; a place to work, to earn, to live.

At night gully winds scoured the city and the curtain blew in tatters, dragging on her window ledge. The sound kept her awake, rubbing out the words she might use as they arose. She could never tell him about the child. Marjorie loved the sound of the curtain and fell asleep to its hush. Jessie knew why now. In that stuffy little house it reminded her of the sea. In her young life she had seen it once. Now Jessie knew she would have to learn to hear the waves in that threadbare scrape.

Lying in bed at night she heard Pamela lose her temper with Marjorie. And you can't help, you can't intercede.

Pamela was dry resignation and dry devotion. Stephen, away trying to get work, had sent home little of his wages. But Pamela merely lit a cigarette, and, sitting at the table in the kitchen, the mean envelope before her, sighed and poured herself another cup of tea. She had the sort of mouth that looked as though it had bled a little at the corners. Her eyes would never change course even in flood.

Jessie knew what the shouting was about. Marjorie, as usual, wanted to sleep in her parents' room with her mother as her small brother Edward did. She stood defiantly in the doorway, waving her arm at the baby's cot, her voice close to tears. Hearing the baby stir, Pamela finally flew at Marjorie with slaps and insults to drive her from the room, and, then holding her by one arm, pushed her back into her own bed and pulled the blankets up to the sobbing child's chin.

A moment later, Marjorie, still shaking with sobs, climbed into Jessie's bed and put her arms around Jessie's neck.

What was it like to be Marjorie? What was it like to be Pamela? At other times, Marjorie sat, heavy on her mother's lap, her arms around her mother's neck, settling an imprint into the wax of her mother's flesh, a seal that ensured that the slaps that were aimed at the child's legs were not ever dangerous.

How much, Jessie thought drowsily, her arms around Marjorie, how much, to one as small as Marjorie, was everyday life dependent on the patience of those arms that could slap and strike in a sudden rage, and yet hold and stroke, stroke away any wound or ache.

In a few months she would have to have arms like Pamela's. That would be her future: that heaviness that crept up week by week towards her heart.

Futures.

Stephen planned futures for himself. Sometimes he would sit, as men sat, on the front step of the house, lazily watching his daughter playing with the children from next door. He would be sitting there when she left for work. The children played a game where they jumped off the edge of the narrow footpath and back again in one quick movement. The children's shouting activity seemed to make the man in the doorway even more still. Sometimes he would sit for an hour without moving except, in summer, to move away the flies. Each of the little houses in the lane had a picket fence along the front of the verandah; there were no gardens. At Stephen's house the pickets had been eaten away at the bottom so that they swang free, kept in place only by the top horizontal timber. The children liked to push them, one eye on their father's gaze, shaking the whole structure.

After living in the lane for two years Stephen knew all the children though he never closely watched them playing. If a fight broke out he would merely watch and never intervene. The older children roamed all over the west end of the city. The toddlers were supposed to stay within the lane. There were days when all the activity would happily occur at the end of the cul-de-sac so that the younger children could, at a distance, watch transfixed the secret schemes of the grown children. But on other days the older children would desert the lane and play in the wide street beyond. Then looking down the lane, you would see in a ragged line, the younger children, eyes as large as the sores on their cheeks, desperate to discover the world of the city, the world of the older children and yet conscious of their mothers who might at any moment emerge from the door and shout with energy across the gutters, over the heads of the slouching men as if they were spirits that a woman might walk through as easily as she now stepped over.

Between each cottage and its neighbour was a panel of wood that meant each verandah was partitioned off from the next. Further down the lane and in the next lane and the next, all across the city, other men sat, silent also, on their doorsteps or on broken-down chairs. They didn't talk. Occasionally they might light a pipe, luxuriating in the ease of the smoke, but they rarely spoke to each other and though each knew the others were sitting there, they still sat as though alone.

Mrs Annabel Madingley liked everything at Montrose to be in the best of taste. Nothing should clash.

She was known throughout every circle in the city as a woman of refinement. More than one husband, the sort of middle-aged husband who comes through a large well-ordered house where children are conveniently at a distance, battling with a nurse-maid behind thick walls and well-polished shut doors, more than one husband coming to kiss his wife goodbye at nine in the morning had found her quite taut with envy over some long report in the city's newspaper (and this newspaper always reported such things at length) of Mrs Madingley's floral arrangements for a ball, her pronouncements on art or her newest impulse for redecorating one of the many large airy rooms in Montrose.

Mr Madingley was large and forgiving. He stood a long way above his tiny, withered wife, hardly seeming to hear her requests for this or this to be altered in the house. He never really needed to listen in any case Jessie noticed: his wealth was so immense that her requests were as ineffectual as a baby's exploration on Christmas morning; one gift might be unpacked and explored but dozens more await exploration and, eventually, some are put away until next year's Christmas.

In a long pre-Raphaelite smock in a light room on the second floor Mrs Madingley would retire every Monday and Wednesday mornings to paint. Jessie discovered from the cook that before her marriage, great things had been prophesied for Annabel Houghton (as she then was). She was known to a wide circle to be highly strung and artistic. Her absence from occasional afternoon teas, which in others would have been considered quite unpardonably rude, had been almost an honour; any hostess with fluffy hair and smooth dress pausing at the sitting-room door to listen to Mrs Houghton's unflustered explanation of why she was late and Annabel not present at all, would, a moment later, convey to the other guests, all on time and already seated, by the very way she sat down and in her tone to the maid, that she, of course understood, that her sympathy was an entreé to a higher world.

Art was not, after all, to be compared to afternoon teas. And this city, Jessie discovered, took art very seriously.

Later, when all the guests had finished their tea, had stopped eating and begun talking, certain of the more sensitive ladies would be allowed morsel by morsel to share the knowledge of what, but of course only in the vaguest terms, Annabel Houghton was painting this week.

Thirty years of marriage and one daughter had not altered this artistic temperament. Occasional small exhibitions of Annabel Madingley's work were held in galleries in the city. One might see one of her prints in the darker part of a long hall of a large house. Of the great future, nothing was ever said.

Ripples and the occasional storm were still caused in the state by Annabel Madingley's pronouncements. With precise regularity she and the patient Mr Madingley would disappear to see their favourite things in France and Italy and her circles would listen eagerly to her accounts of Paris and Sienna, those far off dream-cities, on her return, never questioning her judgements; she was, after all, an artist.

On her last day, dismissed with no reference because of her condition Jessie paused by the door of the studio, which room, alone of all the thirty at Montrose she was not allowed to dust, and stared at the work in progress. It was not the world she ever saw. It was nothing she knew. A small coterie, the élite amongst Mrs Madingley's extensive acquaintance, was sometimes allowed up into the studio. Annabel was so bohemian, so unconventional. It was a charming room, full of light and a studied disorder, which, somehow for all its profusion of canvases, its wide windowsills, pots of geraniums and the avante garde, angular prints here and there on the walls (walls which were, daringly, butterfly yellow), suggested to Jessie as she stood at the door with the hard smell of oil paint around her, a shop window, dusty and unchanged for years in some dying country town.

The rest of the rooms at Montrose were like a beautiful museum, full of preserved life. Precious things stood about in the polished silence; there was everywhere the perfect order, luxury and cleanliness that is only ever found in the houses of the very rich and only there, in the rooms forbidden to the children. In an hour she would be free to walk out into the sun. Somewhere, deep within the house, she thought in the silence as she dusted for the last time, you might come across the king and his wife, mummified, remote, golden, at the heart of all their treasure, their eyes lapis lazuli blue, and forever gazing upwards.

Telling Pamela proved to be easy though she could not understand why.

Are some women just born sensible she wondered looking at Pamela's shapeless cardigan, her old floral dress, the feet in slippers? Any peace I've found always needed travelling; it would be the result of doubt and irresolution, or being told. Pamela will go on having babies and looking after Stephen, her whole life will be spent clearing a space: day by day, organizing, feeding, tidying; beating back grease, dirty clothes, hunger; keeping beds dry, floors swept, hands washed, clearing a space. And that space is for others, for other lives.

'Well where's my tea then?'

She looked at Jessie dreaming and sighed.

'There's not much sugar left you know.'

She sighed again and Jessie realized it was the sound of her life; as others might laugh or gasp, she would sigh.

Jessie poured tea for them both and then added water to the pot.

'They say,' she began. 'They say there's jobs coming up after

Christmas, in the port. That things will look up. That we've passed the worst.'

'They've said that before.' There was silence. Bit by bit they were watching the city die. Colin had never written. He had left, the Misses wrote, without so much as a word.

Sitting on the bed in the heat of the evening, Jessie looked down at her belly before pulling her night-dress over her head. It was a white dome, hard-packed between her legs and her breasts. In the middle, like the faded knob on the end of a lemon, her navel bulged outwards. Long, long ago that navel had been a depression in the centre of her stomach between the twin ridges of her hips. Now her hips had disappeared where the balloon began and her navel bulged out.

How long had she been pregnant? Oh, part of her of course knew exactly how long, could count off on her hands or in her head the months in their different colours, the pink April, red May and darkening green of June and July. But that wasn't what she meant. She had come to accept this bulge. She slept curled around it. She walked, rolling behind it now with an easy, slow gait, head back. All the strangeness she had once felt had disappeared. Her reflection in a window no longer startled her. She never stopped any more to look at herself in the mirror. It seemed the shape she was, nothing more.

In the beginning she had felt her belly might burst with the force behind it. Something hard had pushed at her waist from behind her skin. Every week she had felt she could not grow any larger. But now, her skin stretched in front of her, she felt quite slender. She started when the woman in the shop at the corner remarked kindly on her size. She felt quite small, quite easy, quite normal. She had always been this size. She had always been pregnant.

At first she had spent hours alone at night tracing the baby's every movement beneath her skin, excited and startled by the dim shuffling and knocking, feeling the movements as a pull, a mystery like finding a survivor buried deep in a mine. But now she fell asleep even as her stomach awoke to thuds and claws, now she dreamt around and over the soft heel that trawled nightly past her ribs.

She pulled the nightie slowly over her head. Every night she would think now . . . or now.

It seemed to take forever, having a baby, and she hadn't anticipated that it would, imagining cries and shrieks, feet racing, water rushing into bubbles.

But not this. She lay in the bare room, cleaner than any room she ever remembered, gazing up at the light above her on the impossibly white ceiling. She stared at the light for a long time, knowing that it would remain a light but that staring at it brought some purpose into any other form of looking. After that she knew she would stare out of the window. That was a diversion; to stare at the scalloped edge of the blind and count the scallops, dividing the clouds beneath into the measures of the blind. Of course, the real pleasure was the cold grey nullity of the sky in the square blankness of the window.

Every now and then a starched white sister would appear and listen to her tummy with a trumpet shaped like a child's toy. What could be stranger than that angry face – she was a spinster – the child's toy and the huge white belly being watched and probed. And yet she heard more than Jessie who heard nothing. Sisters would snap the trumpet back into its special holder and walk away after listening. One was kind enough to tell her everything was good. But Jessie lay there lost and abandoned in the white empty room; alone, bored and removed from time. The creature inside her was her only company, moving to its own mysterious rhythms, keeping her awake at night, orchestrating her skin at meals, conducting its hands when she passed water to her infinite chagrin. She knew it would arrive soon and part of her knew that things would not be the same again. But like the child within, that change seemed a distant and unattainable possibility, not something real. Reality was the dullness of night and day, herself sitting in a puddle in McBrides hospital, waiting.

And then all of a sudden as she watched the night sky crotchet itself to the dullness of the blind's edge, she felt a pain reach around the girdle of her hips, so wicked in its grasp, that she was lost in a black descent.

And afterwards? Afterwards when she surfaced, bewildered in the dark, in another bed, without the baby whose cry she dimly remembered through all that pain and terror, she stared out into the dark and fell asleep again, bewildered beyond the unfamiliar territory of a room she had never seen and without guides or maps to the inferno that had brought her here.

Next time she awoke it was morning and a weak light was staining the white quilt of her bed. A soft sound and she turned her head to find that she was not alone. Another two women were sleeping on either side of her, mouths open, hair tousled, sleeping the sleep of the desperate, those who cling to spars of time to save themselves from drowning, from the grey depths of demanded wakefulness.

Half awake, she allowed her eyes to roam around the ugliness of the room, a room that didn't try to do anything except emphasize its ugliness, that tried to appear plain despite its spacious dimensions.

Dozing off she was awakened by a voice.

'I'm Eileen, what did you have?'

The other woman was Rose.

By the end of that day they had talked their way forward into details that grew around each of them and made the birth of their children into starry heights, myths that could be retold without memory or pain.

Birth resolved itself into a series of chapters, anecdotes long in the telling. When she looked back she found she could put together what had happened bit by bit, so that the beginning became a slow passage without connection to life at either end, a removal to a time of terror and pain so great that she couldn't explain how it fitted into the rest of the ordinary world, an episode of suffering that came and came again and yet would not end. It was a time of terror, repeated evil, that stormed and then left to storm again, a pit of pain that would tumble you down, the moment you began to try to climb out so that you started bent and hopeless from the bottom of the pit. Some powerful stranger visited you. You might twist and turn and cry out but no one would come. A strange face would come and observe you and then glance at her own watch while the stranger besieged you twice. And then you were given a pat and the nurse marched out again.

About the end, when the baby was finally born she could find no words for that cruel merry-go-round of pain, a whirlwind of agony and confusion with herself writhing at the centre not understanding and not understood.

When the baby was born it was as though everything changed.

She could lie there, merely gasping, stilled by the wonder of the baby's presence and by her return to the world where pain could be held at arm's length and examined; under the toe a thorn or a finger cut on a tin opener bleeding a little life away. But in some strange mist she saw the baby, crying, rolling, helpless, beating the air with its screams of rage; herself before it was born, as though in giving birth she had released some spirit and freed herself from its power.

In the telling, one voice after another, none of this was ever told. And yet they were frank and spared each other nothing. But each part of their labour once told was retold over the years to any other woman, with the parts and patterns routine in the telling, the words known off by heart, until in the relating nothing could surprise or shock, the pain folded away and buried, losing its power.

All the time she was in hospital she never learnt what the noise was.

She awoke one morning in the dark and thought she had just escaped, changing shape like a cloud in drifts from a dream where there had been some explosion or roar, the world crashing about her sleeping ears. But then as she lay there trying to finger her sense of time and objects, she felt herself drift away into exhaustion, her body lowered suddenly up and down and then down without cease like a bucket that jerks and slips and finally falls into a well of unknown depths. All the strands of wakefulness spun into disorder, a rope that frayed apart and let her fall.

Next night she was awake, or half awake, trying to keep her daughter from falling asleep at the breast. Any minute now the sister would march in and wheel the baby away. It amazed her that they could march about, immaculate in their shoes and uniform and caps in the early hours of the morning, while she and the other women lay, hair disordered, beds stale, night-dresses sweet with leaking milk. And yet in they would come and wheel out all three babies with a flourish, pushing the platoon of cots as though it was wrong that babies had to come out of the distant nursery at all.

Already she loved the baby with a passion that arrived in sudden gusts, like an uncertain wind, now from the north, now from the south. You felt quite calm one minute, quite balanced, grounded with each foot in the easy practicalities, nappies, feeds. But all of a sudden the baby might frown and twist its head, fracture into red tears and you would yourself be in a gale, unbraced and skewwiff, hours later, tears dripping into your tea, the memory of that thirst to comfort suddenly tasted in the throat.

Staring down at the little head she heard the noise again and then again and knew it was not a dream. It sounded as though the hospital knew the day had appeared, far off, and now it shook itself, huge in all its sleeping limbs, wards and corridors stirred and shifted, padded out to salute the return of light.

The next moment the sister appeared and took the baby, Colin's child, away. She had named her Veronica. Interrupted, the baby appeared not even to notice, that it was being taken from its mother's arms. She heard Eileen whisper something quick and furtive before her baby too was taken. They never had the babies except for feeds. When Rose had asked, had dared to ask to see hers there had been a shocked reproof. Rose would spoil her child.

Once, losing her way on her awkward legs, Jessie had found the nursery. The door was shut. In the distance sealed off behind glass, she saw all the cots and between one step and the next, had seen even at this distance the tiny face of her own child, staring out at nothing. Nothing could be done. She had to walk on, alone, though her arms ached to hold the child. Veronica had to stay, alone, uncomforted whether awake or crying. That was the hospital rule. You fitted into the rules and cried one at a time at night, the sound muffled by a pillow over your head, Eileen last night, Rose tomorrow.

By the time she left the hospital, weeks later after walking some great uncountable corridor of time, lost from everything, she knew the sound in the night and accepted it as a part of the night. It was a boilerhouse, she supposed. But in her heart she knew that the hospital awoke with the sound. By the time she left she knew that it was not the padding out of a free spirit that roared at the sun yolked to the horizon. Like the bandaged moment when she saw her child, separated and barred like a calf at the saleyards, she recognized in the sound an innocent beast, caged beyond pity, that every night in the longest hour would shuffle awake, patrol the stale stretches of its cage and then, tears on the fur of its nose, would rush and assault the bars, hoofs on iron, shaking with hopeless pain against the cage, the rules.

She went home to the cottage where Pamela nursed a new baby only a month older than her small daughter. Stephen carried the bassinet into Jessie's room. Veronica was tightly asleep, so absent from the room that it was difficult not to feel she had judged the world and returned to some other distant place. Stephen grinned she noticed, irritated. Why shouldn't she want to look immediately into the little face?

They offered her a cup of tea and she was so overcome by tiredness that she hardly heard. In the kitchen Stephen sat with his head on his arm with Pamela rubbing his hair.

'I'm going to bed.' They nodded; she crawled under the quilt and into blackness.

Hours later she awoke. The room was black, the house silent.

'Where am I?' she thought. Was this the hospital she wondered, befuddled, remembering the smell of disinfectant, the white linen, the blood and the endless crying of most of the babies, so distressing and so relentless that tears would spring to her eyes even as her own daughter slept. But there was silence here. Ah, she was at the cottage, and, as this thought took hold, her body relaxed.

But Veronica, she was here! She stiffened, held her breath and heard faintly the quick puff of breath from the floor beside her pillow. This so relaxed her that she fell half asleep immediately. Minutes later she was aware of a light in the kitchen and of Pamela hurrying down the hall with Kenneth in one arm. He was crying in a loud practised way.

She heard his crying from behind the kitchen door which Pamela had shut, then heard the clatter of a saucepan on the stove. Suddenly the crying stopped. Silence, through which, as she lay half asleep, Jessie could hear the different breath of Veronica and Marjorie and, listening now, even further away, the breath of Stephen and Edward from the front room.

Needing to go outside she put on a cardigan and walked down the hall in the dark.

Pamela sat at the table, her feet stretched towards the stove, Kenneth, in one arm, red from the warmth of milk that he was circled around. Pamela had her eyes shut; she jumped when Jessie crept through and, opening her eyes, smiled.

From the laundry outside, you could see the backs of dozens of other cottages, old fences and rusty iron, sheds and sleep-outs, whitened by the dead light of the moon. She heard the chain of a dog drag on the ground, a small whisper of sound in the silence that lay over the vast sleeping city. She had never woken in the night before Veronica's birth. In the warmth of the kitchen Kenneth had finished and Pamela was changing his nappy on the table. Jessie put the bottles in the sink and they smiled without talking.

Hearing, suddenly, Veronica's cry, so different from Kenneth's, she rushed up the hall only barely conscious of Pamela following to her own room. Nothing could wrack her like that sound. It was a line she could not resist; Veronica could summon her on the hooks of her short cries. Mumbling to the baby, she lit the candle and climbed into bed, resting the taut body on the quilt next to the wall as she undid the front of her night-dress and offered her breast to the hunting mouth. The baby leapt and was silent.

Moths appeared around the candle flame. She had a sudden image, not only of Pamela and herself, awake in the dead of the night, but also of hundreds of other mothers, somewhere out there in the vast closed-down city, fumbling half asleep in different dim-lit rooms and then sitting much as she sat, motionless yet intent, not awake and yet not asleep, lost in the small breath on their arms, yet at the same time hearing and knowing a world the sleeping city never would.

As she felt the silence extend into minutes and felt Veronica's head drowse on her arm, she knew the boundaries of her world diminished to this small galaxy of cries and silences, knew why the reel of the baby's voice could so swiftly move her feet, and why she circled, held, around that light, knew herself glad to burn her wings in the candle of the child.

10

Colin's child, flesh of her flesh.

The baby's cries filled every part of the house. You could walk away but the sound hunted you wherever you went. Another person could shout at you and it would not have half the effect of the baby's thin cry. It followed you around the house, a swarm of bees that clouded every moment, threatening the light. Milk would seethe in your breasts, like the stinging of bees, an echo of the baby's cry. It was like tears she supposed. Often as she walked towards the little cot, milk would splash onto her feet, washing off the dust in some homage that she could not control.

Did she love Veronica? There were moments after hours of crying when she hated the clouding of her days. Moments when she attended to the baby in silence, longing for it to sleep, feeling nothing. They would retire like armies after battle.

Then she would creep in and see the baby asleep in her cot, the roundness of her head, and feel her arms ache to hold her again.

She had left the little port only to discover another kind of death. What was the life of the city? Only when dying became destruction would it grow and renew itself. Everywhere babies were born to anxious parents, carried into shabby houses and crowded out, awkward fathers too much about. The city remained the same and so it grew old and unkempt, begrimed, able only to mumble, forgetting, unable to wash or dress. With nothing in the present to celebrate, bunting and tinsel appeared to commemorate the Armistice. The city was a big house on a hill but also a wall peeling paint, a boarded-up window, a lean-to, where grateful for shelter, behind rags dark with dirt that let in air but blocked the light, from stained mattresses, families awakened to another day, scratching; a day of getting by, a day exactly like the day before and all the other days before that, which in the end turned into years without change.

When it rained water dripped into the room where Jessie slept with Veronica and Marjorie. Nothing could be done; to have the roof repaired would cost the earth. Stephen talked quietly every night with Pamela and one morning after breakfast he announced he intended to go interstate to look for work.

'I'll never get it here. But up north . . .' He smiled at the sad, disbelieving faces. Pamela who had seen him go and return before, turned away.

'Will you tell him to come here if you see him?' Jessie asked at the gate.

He looked at her and smiled without answering.

She had never felt angry with him in her life, she realized, until that moment. 'Well, will you?'

Still he was silent. He turned away. 'Why don't you forget him, Jess,' he said in his old voice, his little boy voice full of charm.

She had to smile. 'How can I?'

'What about Veronica?' she asked exasperated into the silence.

'What about her?'

She stared at him, lost for words until he shrugged.

'I'll tell him,' he said shortly.

You were a ship not far from shore, held by rope, a prisoner of that continent of furious need. You might drift a little on the calm current of the baby's sleep. But always there was the rope.

Desperate and trembling with hunger, Veronica was picked up, her mouth working as Jessie, cradling her, sat down on the step that led into the kitchen. Somewhere, outside, Marjorie and Edward roamed the small space between the house and the shed. Jessie liked sitting on the step, feeling the air and space, the sense of not being in the dark crowded house, liking to watch the shadows of the peach tree leaning over from the next yard, close enough she thought, to shout if Edward and Marjorie quarrelled.

She turned from looking outside. Great tears lay untrustingly around the baby's eyes, but already her face was losing that ruined crumpled look, and becoming as she sucked, the perfect baby's face again, her head sinking softer onto Jessie's arm. Her eyes had changed as if in reproach from blue to Colin's green reminding her when she least needed it of his eternal absence. How many times every day did she sit like this with Veronica, each feed following the other with quickness, inexorable, the only way to end pain, renew peace between the two of them. Short gaps of time could be snatched between this real business, washing or sleep might be begun always only to be left, unfinished; her hands accomplishing as little as the baby's hands did, waving, jerking, moving, alive and insistent, reaching towards Jessie as she bent over the cot or rushing past, batting at motes in the sun.

Sitting like this, she thought of Colin.

A long time ago she had felt that there were choices, that

she might be free to go one way or another although she had never known, where any of the ways would in the end lead. Perhaps to here. That had been childhood; the future seeming to be as clear and delicate as the landscapes in the books Miss Symes had allowed her; an endless sky and one gently winding road to an unexplored horizon full of rewards for the right and brave. But even after that feeling had changed so many years ago, she had still felt that her choices were not always set. Even after she began working, she might set down trays with grace, let tea brew just long enough or slam doors and twitch curtains so that the rings pulled on the rod with a jerking sound, like someone in tears. Even knowing she would always work, she still had space to improvise, to stay silent or to smile, or even, as she had finally done from Montrose, to walk out past the scenery, off the stage with only one backward glance to where the others still stood, in profile curiously unlike people, turned and always turning towards some sun, like weak-stemmed flowers.

Veronica had finished.

She put the little head up on her shoulder. Sometimes when she looked at her own hands, when Veronica was asleep, she was startled to realize that the brown skin was exactly like her own.

It was Veronica's skin she had, for a moment's forgetfulness, been seeing instead of her own; so much of every day was spent looking at the baby's skin, the baby's face.

Veronica brought her the future and the present now with directions and applause from the moment she stirred in the bassinet in the mornings until the hour at night when she finally let oblivion coil around her short limbs, her breath sleeping on the air as you listened at the door. There were no choices. She would have to forget Colin.

Out of the blue, Stephen appeared at the front door and walked down the hall to the kitchen with his bag and cigarettes. Whatever Pamela or I are doing he would stay sitting at the table, she thought, one hand holding a cigarette or a cup of tea. He doesn't even greet the children.

Today rain hemmed in the rows of cottages, making the kitchen dark with noise and children. The babies filled the house, seeming always to be in tears one after the other.

'Any luck?' Jessie asked with ritual care.

'What do you think?' Pamela stirred cereal for Kenneth with even strokes.

Waiting for Veronica to wake, Jessie watched Edward. He bounced, holding onto the steps, entertaining her. He climbed to his feet by pulling on her skirt as she sat in the chair, then wobbled and fell as the material came towards him too easily. His cries ballooned out, big in the small room. Jessie picked him up, knowing his cries tugged at Pamela where she had no hands, and poured a cup of tea for them both, moving the whole room towards silence and peace by distracting Edward with the teapot's emergence from under the tea-cosy.

It lasted a few seconds, the rain drumming into the moment louder than ever, and then Veronica began to cry from her room off the hallway. His lot to be put down, half comforted, Edward crawled after Jessie as she walked into the cold to get Veronica and bring her back to the one warm room.

Stephen began his story to the half-listening Pamela. Like any story, Jessie thought as she put Veronica on the table and began to heat the cereal, to be properly told it would need the teller to move out from the wall, to take a deep breath and advance into the centre, to use space and create wonder so that the listener would become entranced, would hear eventually, where there was silence, in the story-teller's involvement, his daring to wear his heart on his sleeve, that distant beating, drums. But when Stephen told a story, Jessie thought suddenly, you couldn't tell where he was; any approach made to him would mean retreat, certainly masked by laughter but still, disappearance, the sight perhaps of a feeler waving from under the skirting, but most of all watchfulness, detachment.

And all this accompanied by that gay smile she was coming to hate.

So you came full circle in the end she thought.

You were taken away from everything you had been before. In part it was the sheer pressure of the days, the endless need to be there, on your feet, the baby learning the sound and definition of the world from the face so often reflected in its own eyes.

She kept her watch beside her when she fed the baby, taking it off so that the metal face would not mark the baby's head. She must time the feeds they had told her in the hospital, and she did for the first couple of months. It seemed part of a discovery that whereas before time had been her own, now it was something that the baby gave.

Today Veronica was four months old. It seemed only a brief night since she was born. She stared down at the baby who wriggled with delight, smiling around a tongue covered in bubbles. Sounds flowed from the baby's mouth in an airy thread; she chewed on the careless translucence, that web of cries.

She had forgotten her watch and remembered now that it lay carelessly close to the washtub. The baby broke into a smile, unabashed by her frown.

'You know, don't you, don't you?' she whispered. 'Now I'll just have to let you decide.' Why was the watch necessary at all she wondered staring down at the baby's feet. She thought of the giant black wands on the face of the Post Office clock, half a mile away in the centre of the city. Every night you could count the quarter hours against its chime. It kept a walking pace, the regular time of dark-suited clerks, office doors and lunch hours, bite by bite. In summer it felled the heat, in winter, the wind. When she had first come to the city she had heard its chime at 6 a.m. knowing she would have to set in motion all the movements that ended only when she knocked at the kitchen door of Montrose to work. The Post Office clock with its giant voice marched to work with the city.

But now, she realized, at home with this child, she never heard those easy bells, those hours cut into quarters, every one. Her time was endless and too short. It moved and bent, without flow or cause. Sometimes there would be no time to do anything before the child called, and then next day the baby would sleep hour after hour, the silence leaving her alone and surprised, listening to the wall of starlings and street noise for that voice, that cry.

How slowly the child grew. And yet the time since her birth had been quicker months than she had ever known.

A child owns the time she thought. Once she herself had owned a summer's length, centuries of warmth beside the river, long ago with Stephen. You came full circle. And now she was not a child, everything was turned over, forever upside down, now all she could hold in her hands were the seconds, the grains her child trickled through the narrow spaces, the hourglass of her days.

Under the city monuments the dignitaries stood, the sun collecting in the dark wool of their suits. Sweat stained collars. By nightfall extravagant wreaths were dying, petal by a thousand petals, turning overnight into a ruin, stamen and calyx baked into clay.

In the cottage in the city there had not been a letter or money for weeks. Stephen had gone and come back again a dozen times by the autumn.

Jessie and Pamela decided. And so she went once again to apply for a position as part-time help in a large house this time in one of the eastern suburbs. Approaching the high cast-iron gates she thought only of the money she might earn. The house set itself up as they all did, to impose. Its windows faced west towards the city. It was far and away the biggest house in the street, two-storeyed with wide high verandahs and French doors on three sides. She sighed thinking of the life such houses meant. Anyone who felt, gazing out at the sweeping lawns, the tall pines or the tennis court that he wanted to stroll about, to flick the ash from his cigar absentmindedly over the verandahs or the long flowerbeds, only had to put his hand on the large brass door-knob and he would be free. There would be someone to sweep it up for him.

At the back on the eastern side of the house were the vegetable gardens and fruit trees. The gravelled drive swept around the back of the house where there was a seat, a tap, a dog's kennel – all the sorts of things usually found at the back doors of large houses she thought; the sort of things that tell you you're at the right entrance. She knocked in the clear spring sunshine. Veronica squatted down to pick up pieces of gravel as the door opened.

Mrs Ford was a beach of pebbles the way other people have faces of sand. There was something about such a large freckled face, such an expansive body that Jessie liked; it wouldn't shift easily with the tides.

'Never married, Mrs Ford. I would have to have her with me some days.'

The child was listening from her lap. What did she know? What did children ever know?

'I like your face. If she's good, then.'

Mrs Ford studied the references on the table.

'Why did you leave Montrose. Apart from – ?'

Jessie nodded. Mrs Ford laughed.

'Annabel always bores me stiff.' The flesh on her arms shook and her body moved inside her dress. It would have to be some other younger you, to be stiff Jessie thought. She smiled and

Veronica, in her best white dress (from a smaller Marjorie), twisted around to look at her mother's face.

We live in a world of children, Pamela and I, she thought.

Kenneth's world waited just beyond the end of his short fingers. It was not something to be looked at but something to be squeezed, banged and eaten. Marjorie might go off to a far corner of the yard and dig in the dirt with a peg, slyly eating gravel when she thought you were not watching, but when she was digging she muttered to herself a long story, full of violence, compromise and development, her voice rising and falling so that in the end the dirt and the digging would be forgotten while the story rose all around her bare legs and grubby arms and shone on her face.

But Kenneth, the baby, could invent no world for himself because the world was always there; ready to bite or fall around him, his to explore.

He set out from the kitchen now, as Jessie watched, dragging himself clumsily, all large nappy and pilchers. He went erratically sideways because he could not yet walk. Half way to the door he discovered an old onion skin and stopped, swivelling upright, straight-backed, pyramid shaped, serious investigator-baby, his fat legs bent to balance himself, both hands free to pull the fragment of skin and then to put it, seriously, into his wet mouth.

Jessie knew she was not the right person for Kenneth. She took the onion skin from his mouth and he did not protest as she gave him a cup instead. He even made a little joke for her pretending to drink from the empty cup, making her laugh. He was that sort of baby. Your face would always mirror his wide-eyed laughing gaze, she thought. He moved towards the door, tumbled as he always did over the step, and kept on going like a crab, a stoic shambling to the leaves under the peach tree. There was no window in the kitchen and they always left the door open on warm days. Jessie moved a chair to the step, watching alone on a Saturday morning, Veronica sleeping, contained in the cot in the middle room, Pamela roaming the city in search of cheap pitted fruit, mutton with a green skin.

Marjorie flew over Kenneth's wondering head from the far corner of the yard.

'Can I sit on y' lap Auntie Jess?'

'Come on, then.'

A four-year-old bundle of bony limbs compared to Kenneth's softness, she was already climbing up. The world where one might sit alone slipped further away, before she had even finished speaking. You're the oldest child and you know you're no longer charming but you've learnt to charm, Jessie thought, as the child turned with a smile of gratitude not insincere for being practised and perfect.

Kenneth had found a stick and was clever with it. Wanting Jessie to see his cleverness he banged it on the fence and then looked up at her. He would laugh she knew, if she called out to him. There was a small space of sun and dirt between them. Once long ago I sat in the stones and dirt, another country without speech, she thought. An aunt, a mother she called to him as he sat under the leafy branches. When he laughs he's reaching out over all the sun and dirt that could exist between us, taking me into his speechless world since he can't yet join me and the child, sitting, talking.

Only Pamela was the right person for him, she thought suddenly. Never would it matter to him that Pamela's face was unwashed or crumpled, he knew hers was the only face for him, the face that defined all others, the only face that would answer his every cry with words, while others misunderstood his attempts, the face that was there for him in his soft unintelligible world and the only face that would help him build, word by word, a path of speech and guide him along it back into that other world, the world she had left to be with him, the talking world of human life.

George Ford was an invalid, nearly blind. I'm his eyes she thought, amazed, reading the paper to him on her first morning.

His bedroom was a large upstairs room with a balcony. If you looked west she thought you might see the city. Tomorrow, she decided, I'll go across to the window when I first come in, partly to pull back the curtains so that I could see to read, and partly to give him a chance to pretend that he's not been dozing. Because he was even now, again as she began the editorial. Was he dying? She looked at the sediment on his cheeks, the wrinkled sand left by a river that would never again flood. He was older than anyone she had ever seen. I'll be like that one day she thought; nothing will stop my days.

She went to the window stepping to the rock of his strident sleep. Today the sky was clear and windswept. Half the city could be glimpsed; it looked a place where things might be happening. The sedate house seemed distant from any concerns, marooned by its large gardens and drives. The city was a mirage, vague shapes miles away. Between the city and the house, a few gum trees had survived all the spreading of roads and houses so that now in the September winds they could glint and twist high above the pattern of roofs.

There was a cough. She went to the bed. The old man glanced up. She knew he could see only light and dark but she smiled as she sat down. My voice is a lifeline she thought and I'm a stranger to him. He'll never even know what I look like. And yet he clutches the sheets with a child's candour and smiles with a mouth that could still be hurt. What has life been to make this? He had once been well known, she knew only that.

'Without the daily paper he would have died long ago' she remembered Mrs Ford telling her on the day of the interview.

She went on reading while the old man sat, alert and eager, his white-haired throat trembling each time he swallowed. An hour passed. Debates, installations, accidents and incidents all found her voice. She folded the paper in half so that it was easier to hold. Far-off through the silence, she heard Veronica begin to cry from her room next to the kitchen.

'I've got to go Sir.' He smiled, the blind face nodded.

I go from old to young, she thought, folding the paper and putting it next to the bed. At the door she stopped and looked back. He was taking the paper in one trembling hand. He smoothed it out and then lay leaning against the pillows for a long time. Eventually he picked up the paper in both hands and brought it up to an inch or two of his failed eyes, willing them to see what I've read, but what no voice could ever convey she mused, wanting in his world of light and dark, despite having had all the black and white print read to him, to feel that old elixir, the implications, the shades of grey. But what made that face, already ancient, so alive? She had seen younger faces already closer to death.

Making jam with Mrs Ford she found the answer had appeared, like all truths, when it would, not when you asked.

'I expect you to take half a dozen of these off our hands Jess.' Mrs Ford stirred comfortably, leaning her bulk against the stove. Jessie paused, then put the jars in her hands next to the pan.

On the floor at the other end of the room Veronica banged a collection of lids together, the sound jarring in the heat, despite the size of the kitchen.

Jessie felt a moment of irritation and then realized the offer was not intended to insult. It was as much a part of Mrs Ford as the superfluity of jars that stood filled on the kitchen table or the number of times she went upstairs on her swollen heavy legs to console her husband in his terrible relegation from the world of politics to blindness and paralysis. How loved the frail old man had been she thought. Knowing his irritability and

198

the pride that made him refuse to be fed (then watch, seeing horridly through his opaque sight how much food had to be quietly wiped off his pyjamas and the quilt), Mrs Ford, without complaint, allowed him still the dignity of eating alone.

They had loved each other, that fat woman and that blind man. That was the answer.

They survived together, the women, sharing everything that winter. They heard once from Stephen but he sent no money. They relied on Jessie for everything. There were no treats or feasts.

'I don't know how you put up with him,' Jessie burst out one evening. They were sitting in the kitchen. Pamela sighed.

'What else can I do?'

But Jessie was not satisfied. It was like a splinter under the skin, to end its nagging you had to gouge with a needle, injure yourself to heal. She sat down at the table litigant and judge opposite Pamela.

'When I first knew him he sat with his arm around me night after night at the kitchen table where I worked. He would run his fingers up and down my bare arm looking at my face. Eventually he would let his arm fall away. He was very shy. After a while I missed his face.'

She got up and laughed.

'But he doesn't even care about them,' Jessie said jerking her head towards the front room where the children slept.

'You know what he'd say? Men are just little boys.' Pamela turned away in contempt. 'Well, what can I do. I married him. That's the way it is.'

He might stay a little boy Jessie thought. Then she realized. She had been a child herself when he was young.

She sat alone after Pamela had gone to bed staring at the faded pattern on the table. It was not something you noticed or liked, it was just there every day. The way it is. She wasn't like Pamela. She couldn't believe Stephen was the person she had loved all her life.

For after all what was he? A man who drifted without caring in and out of their lives. A man who didn't care for his own children. A man who felt nothing.

Outside she heard the wind hunting leaves across the roof. It blew from the south, bringing the coldness of the sea across the thin heat of the land, blowing all the way from the shore she had walked along as a child with an adored brother.

She didn't know how long she sat listening to the wind. It wouldn't stop. It blew from somewhere so distant that she couldn't begin to imagine how cold it was. It blew forever and now sucked at her door with the oldest voice in the world.

They had stood on the beach, brother and sister, and he had held a mussel shell and then torn it apart so that the wonderful matching pieces were lost to each other forever. Blood's not thicker than water she thought; in the rain it can be washed to nothing. Something in him had frozen and would never recover. The wind had scratched messages in the sand and only now did she understand what they were.

On a Saturday morning Jessie achieved a petty triumph. She was sitting down, the children were happy, the cats fed.

Pamela was out at the market. They had both slept in, and after Pamela left, Jessie had roused herself, half dressed and tired, and stumbled about the house trying to feed the four children and dress herself. In Pamela's slippers, an old skirt and jumper she cooked bacon and eggs, Saturday's treat, while Marjorie and Edward waited, fighting around the table. Kenneth crawled under the table, and Veronica, who had been smacked, cried sullenly and determinedly in the corner of the kitchen, her nappy, heavy and wet, around her knees.

While she was up in the middle room minutes later, changing

Veronica, Edward spilt his milk. Somehow it missed Kenneth; when Jessie walked in a minute later, he was admiring it dripping onto the floor. She let the cats in to lap up the puddle, wiped the table and gave Veronica a piece of bread and dripping to chew on the step. The eggs had stuck and she scraped the oozing yellow and brittle white into a dish to spoon into Kenneth's waiting mouth. Tea. She'd have to have a cup.

'You kids dress yourselves.' Marjorie and Edward ran up the hall, itching to get to the life of the street where the other children's voices rose like spring shoots of grass through the cold winter.

She gave Kenneth a piece of bread and put on the kettle. Feeling extravagant she turned on the gas jets in the oven to warm up the room. Her feet hurt, coming to life.

Eventually she was able to sit down and drift off on the warmth of the tea, away a little from the rocks of last night's broken sleep. The front door banged behind Marjorie and the younger children chewed contentedly on the step, smearing dripping on their hands. She put the frying pan on the floor, conscious of the cats purring around her legs, and put her feet on the edge of the oven door, feeling the warmth like pain.

Horses in a stall he had said.

Every morning in the early light she went to the corner shop for milk. It was their main expense.

She washed her face and dressed, moving quietly through the spaces of the tiny cottage between the quietness of Pamela and the sleeping babies. If you looked at their faces, she thought, tiptoeing out of Pamela's room with the pennies in her hand, you would see the babies' cheeks covered with a fine pink bloom. They slept bent backwards like cherubim, their hands before their faces on invisible flutes. They slept in a world without thoughts, without the need to forget. But our faces, she thought, looking back at the sleeping Pamela, even by morning are still folded around care, creased with need.

She pulled the door shut without locking it and set off through the alley. There was no one about but the smell of poverty remained.

The dew on the grass looks dirty, she thought glancing through the pinched paling fence on the vacant block at the corner. Yellow light leant at corners, streaking the walls with new angles the colour of old flannel. Fingers of sun lifted new dirt in the glare.

And yet she liked this time of day. Something, even here in the heart of the city, came only with the light of morning. The streets were dirty and the houses poor but the light was new and sweet even as it fell before her into the gutters. Washed-out colour and faded patterns but it's still a dress worth wearing, she thought.

At the corner of the street she slowed to a dawdle. This house had flowers in its garden. She stopped.

All of a sudden, drowning in the thick honey of their scent, she went past her walking pleasure to the halt they brought, feet clamped in the cruel snares of memory.

She had tried after the child's birth to forget. I wanted them both she thought, Stephen and Colin, and I have neither.

Two years ago leaning on the churchyard wall with Colin's gaze falling around her, manna in the dry waste of life, she had wondered about the years between the dates on all those tombstones. What made them good or bad? Then too, there had been freesias flowering in another spring, milk and yellow trumpets at the foot of the wall, sweet triumph that might fell Jericho. There was nothing she loved more than that: the way he had watched the butterfly on her shoulder, perfume in the air around her swimming head.

It would not die, that feeling. I might deny it, she thought, control it, or skirt around it, but like something ordinary, something simple it would never fail, it would disappear only to flower again next year.

Flowers in the basket,
Basket on the bed,
Bed in the chamber,
Chamber in the house,
House in the weedy yard,
Yard in the winding lane,
Lane in the broad street,
Street in the high town,
Town in the city,
City in the kingdom:
This is the key of the kingdom.

He had been right. Life without him had ended. The flowers, small trumpets, had in one moment brought that love back when she believed it dead.

We walk as women walk she thought, a long string of children knotted around us, the youngest in the pusher, a little more protected from the sun. Parcels and vegetables were attached everywhere to the pusher and themselves. On the way home they usually collected Marjorie from the street, her stocky figure, detaching itself from the other children and running zigzag towards them, but today, being Christmas eve, she had wanted to come with them. Usually before they completed the trip home, one of the children would have fallen or quarrelled or had some other reason to need the comfort of arms already used by string bags of cauliflower or brisket. So they came to expect an unloading and reorganization half way between the shops and home, when shoelaces could be retied, truces between rivals enforced or the bullying scolded. The parcels seemed heavier when they bent to pick them up again and they longed for the house to be reached, too tired even to talk to each other by the time they saw the beginning of their street.

Later, hearing only faint murmurs from the two rooms where

the children slept, Jessie and Pamela decorated the Christmas tree in the kitchen. The tree was not large but it was a Christmas tree. It had been given to Marjorie and Edward by the butcher that afternoon, and they had dragged it all the way from the market staining their hands with sour honey, resin that to their delight would not wash off. So now Jessie sat on the floor in the hall cutting long strips of paper which Pamela made into looping chains. The hall was dark apart from the light that fell on them from the kitchen and they had left the front door open so that the gully wind snaked its coolness right through the centre of the house.

In the street there were footsteps.

'Merry Christmas girls.'

'Girls.' Pamela laughed.

'And a Happy New Year.'

'What do you reckon?' Jessie asked as the men moved on.

'Oh, next year!' Pamela laughed. 'Stephen'll come back and go again.'

Jessie was silent. She had loved him once long ago.

Suddenly she was filled with a calm peace. She would find Colin she felt certain. He would one day know he had a child. She would place an advertisement in the paper to find him.

Deciding that Christmas had begun, she gave Pamela her packet of cigarettes and they shared one, sitting on the floor in the half-dark, passing it to each other, the small light flowing between them. We're poor gems, she thought, shining as we could never do in a bigger light, sparkling like riches in the eyes of children.

All of a sudden there was a sound. Kenneth thumped.

'Out of the cot, oh hell,' thought Jessie.

But instead of crying he came slowly out of the bedroom and laughing, swaying, triumphant with achievement, advanced down the hall, not crawling but walking, for the first time, alone, tall, towards the women in the light and behind them, the tree.

'The tree,' she said and held out her arms to the child's steps.